The Burglar's Fate
AND THE DETECTIVES
AN ALLAN PINKERTON DETECTIVE STORY

The Burglar's Fate
AND THE DETECTIVES
An Allan Pinkerton Detective Story

Allan Pinkerton

ÆGYPAN PRESS

1884

Special thanks to Jeroen van Luin, Suzanne Shell, and the Online
Distributed Proofreading Team (which can be found at
http://www.pgdp.net/).

The Burglar's Fate and the Detectives
A publication of
ÆGYPAN PRESS

www.aegypan.com

Preface

In the pages which follow I have narrated a story of actual occurrence. No touch of fiction obscures the truthful recital. The crime which is here detailed was actually committed, and under the circumstances which I have related. The four young men, whose real names are clothed with the charitable mantle of fiction, deliberately perpetrated the deed for which they suffered and today are inmates of a prison. No tint or coloring of the imagination has given a deeper touch to the action of the story, and the process of detection is detailed with all the frankness and truthfulness of an active participant. As a revelation of the certain consequences which follow the perpetration of crime, I send this volume forth, in the fervent hope that those who may read its pages, will glean from this history the lessons of virtue, of honor, and of the strictest integrity. If in the punishment of Eugene Pearson, Dr. Johnson, Newton Edwards and Thomas Duncan, the young men of today, tempted by folly or extravagance, will learn that their condemnation was but the natural and inevitable result of thoughtless crime, and if their experience shall be the means of deterring one young man from the commission of a deed, which the repentance of years will not obliterate, I shall feel that I have not labored in vain. As a true story of detective experience, the actors in which are still living, I give this volume to the world, trusting that its perusal may not fail in its object of interesting and instructing the few or many who may read its pages.

ALLAN PINKERTON

Chapter I

*Geneva — The Robbery — Search for the Burglars — My Agency
Notified.*

Geneva is one of the prettiest and most thriving little towns in the
west. Situated, as it is, in the midst of one of the finest agricultural
districts in the country, its growth has been rapid beyond expectation,
while its social progress has been almost phenomenal. Stretching for
miles in all directions, over a country beautifully interspersed with
gentle elevations and depressions, lie the well-cultivated farms of the
honest tillers of the soil. The farmhouses, which nestle down beneath
the tall trees, present an appearance of comfort and beauty rarely
witnessed, while the commodious and substantial out-buildings evince
the thorough neatness of systematic husbandry. Standing upon a high
knoll, and gazing over the scene upon a bright sunny morning, the eye
lights upon a panorama of rustic splendor that delights the vision and
entrances the senses. The vast fields, with their varied crops, give indications of a sure financial return which the gathered harvests unfailingly
justify, and the rural population of Geneva are, in the main, a community of honest, independent people, who have cheerfully toiled for the
honest competence they so fully enjoy.

Nor is the town dependent alone upon the farmer and the herdsman
for its success in a financial sense. Nature has been bounteous in her
gifts to this locality, and in addition to the fertile and fruitful soil, there
is found imbedded under the surface, great mines of coal, of excellent
quality, and seemingly inexhaustible in quantity. This enterprise alone
affords employment to hundreds of men and boys, who, with their
begrimed faces and brawny arms, toil day and night in the bowels of
the earth for the "black diamonds," which impart warmth and light to
countless happy homes, and materially add to the wealth of the miners.

Numerous manufacturing industries also find a home here. Large
buildings, out of whose huge chimneys the black smoke is pouring forth

in dense volumes, and whose busy wheels and roaring furnace fires, mingled with the sound of scores of ringing hammers, make merry music throughout the day.

On certain days in the week Geneva presents a cheerful and animated appearance. On every hand are heard the sounds of honest toil and the hum of busy trade. Farmers from the surrounding country come in numbers into the village to purchase their necessary supplies and to listen to the news and gossip of the day, and the numerous stores transact a thriving business and reap a handsome profit on their wares.

The old mill, weather-beaten and white with the accumulating flour dust of ages, and with the cobwebs hanging thick and heavy from its dingy rafters, stands near by, and this too is an object of interest to the sturdy farmers of the surrounding country. From morn till night its wheels go round, transmuting the grain into the various articles of consumption for man and beast, and bringing a goodly share of "honest toll" into the coffers of the unimpeachable old miller. The mill is a great place of meeting for the farmers, and the yard in its front is daily filled with teams from the country, whose owners congregate in groups and converse upon topics of general interest, or disperse themselves, while waiting for their "grist," about the town to transact the various matters of business which had brought them hither.

In common with all progressive American towns, Geneva boasts of its school-house, a large brick building, where rosy-cheeked children daily gather to receive the knowledge which is to fit them more thoroughly for the great battle of life, when the years shall have passed and they become men and women.

Here, too, are banking institutions and warehouses, and every element that contributes to the thrift and advancement of a happy, honest, hard-working and prosperous people.

Of its history, but few words are necessary for its relation. Not many years ago it was the home of the red man, whose council fires gleamed through the darkness of the night, and who roamed, free as the air, over the trackless prairie, with no thought of the intruding footsteps of the pale-face, and with no premonition of the mighty changes which the future was to bring forth.

Then came the hardy pioneers — those brave, self-reliant men and women who sought the broad acres of the west, and builded their homes upon the "edge of civilization." From that time began the work of progress and cultivation. Towns, villages and cities sprang up as if under the wand of the magician. Fifty years ago, a small trading post, with its general store, its hand grist-mill, rude blacksmith-shop and the fort. Today, a busy active town, with more than five thousand inhabitants, a hundred business enterprises, great railroad facilities, and every element that conduces to prosperity, honesty and happiness.

Such is Geneva today, a substantial, bustling, thriving and progressive village of the west.

It is a hot, sultry day in August, 18--, and the shrill whistles from the factories have just announced the arrival of six o'clock. Work is suspended for the day, and the army of workmen are preparing for their homes after the labors of the day.

At the little bank in Geneva the day has been an active one. Numerous herders have brought their stock into market, and after disposing of them have deposited their moneys with the steady little institution, in which they have implicit confidence, and through which the financial affairs of the merchants and farmers round about are transacted.

The last depositor has departed, and the door has just been closed. The assistant cashier and a lady clerk are engaged within in settling up the business of the day. At the Geneva bank the hours for business vary with the requirements of the occasion, and very frequently the hour of six arrives ere their customers have all received attention and their wants have been supplied. This had been the case upon this day in August, and breathing a sigh of relief as the last customer took his leave, the front door was locked and the work of balancing up the accounts was begun.

Suddenly, a knock is heard at the outer door, and Mr. Pearson, the assistant cashier, being busily engaged, requested the young lady with him to answer the summons. As she did so, two men, roughly dressed, and with unshaved faces, burst into the room. Closing the door quickly behind them, one of the men seized the young lady from behind and placed his hand upon her mouth. Uttering a piercing scream, the young lady attempted to escape from the grasp upon her, and with her teeth she inflicted several severe wounds upon the ruffianly hand that attempted to smother her cries. In a moment she was knocked down, a gag was placed in her mouth, and she was tied helplessly hand and foot. While this had been transpiring, the other intruder had advanced to the assistant cashier, and in a few moments he too was overpowered, bound and gagged. In less time than is required to tell the story, both of them were lying helpless before their assailants, while the open doors of the bank vault revealed the treasures which had excited the passions of these depraved men, and led to the assault which had just been successfully committed.

No time was to be lost, the alarm might be sounded in a moment, and the thieves, picking up a valise which stood near by, entered the vault, and securing all the available gold, silver and bank-notes, placed them in the satchel and prepared to leave the place.

Before doing so, however, they dragged the helpless bodies of the young man and woman into the despoiled vault, and laying them upon the floor, they deliberately closed the doors and locked them in.

Not a word had been spoken during this entire proceeding, and now, in silence, the two men picked up the satchel, and with an appearance of unconcern upon their faces, passed out of the bank and stood upon the sidewalk.

The streets were filled with men and women hurrying from their work. The sun was shining brightly in the heavens, and into this throng of human beings, all intent upon their own affairs, these bold burglars recklessly plunged, and made their way safely out of the village.

How long the two persons remained in the bank it is impossible to tell; Miss Patton in a deathlike swoon, and Mr. Pearson, in the vain endeavor to extricate himself from the bonds which held him. At length, however, the young man succeeded in freeing himself, and as he did so, the young lady also recovered her consciousness. Calling loudly for help, and beating upon the iron door of their prison, they indulged in the futile hope that someone would hear their cries and come to their rescue.

At last, however, Mr. Pearson succeeded in unscrewing the bolts from the lock upon the inside of the doors of the vault, and in a few minutes thereafter, he leaped out, and dashing through a window, gave the alarm upon the street. The news spread far and wide, and within an hour after the robbery had taken place, the town was alive with an excited populace, and numerous parties were scouring the country in all directions in eager search of the fugitives. All to no avail, however, the desperate burglars were not discovered, and the crest-fallen bank officers contemplated their ruin with sorrowful faces, and with throbbing hearts.

Meanwhile, Miss Patton had been carefully removed to her home, her injuries had been attended to, and surrounded by sympathetic friends, who ministered to her wants, she was slowly recovering from the effects of the severe trial of the afternoon.

An examination of the vault revealed the fact that the robbers had succeeded in obtaining about twenty thousand dollars in gold, silver and currency — all the available funds of the bank, and the loss of which would seriously impair their standing, and which would be keenly felt by everyone interested in its management.

Though sorely crippled by their loss, the bank officials were undismayed, and resolved to take immediate steps for the capture of the criminals, and the recovery of the stolen property. To this end they decided to employ the services of my agency at once, in the full hope that our efforts would be crowned with success. Whether the trust of the directors was well founded, and the result so much desired was achieved, the sequel will show.

Chapter II

The Investigation Begun — John Manning's Visit to Geneva — Eugene Pearson's Story — The Detective's Incredulity — A Miraculous Deliverance With a Ten-Cent Coin.

On the evening of the same day on which this daring robbery occurred, and as I was preparing to leave my agency for the day, a telegram was handed to me by the superintendent of my Chicago office, Mr. Frank Warner. The message read as follows:

"Geneva, August --, 18--.
"Bank robbed today. Twenty thousand dollars taken. Please send or come at once.
"(Signed,) Henry Silby, President"

This was all. There was no detail of particulars, no statement of the means employed, only a simple, concise and urgent appeal for my services. As for myself, realizing the importance of promptness and dispatch in affairs of this nature, and fully appreciating the anxiety of the bank officials, I resolved to answer their call as speedily as possible. But few words of consultation were required for the subject, and in a short time I had selected the man for the preliminary investigation, and requested his presence in my office. John Manning was the operative chosen for this task, an intelligent, shrewd and trusty young man of about thirty years of age, who had been in my employ for a long time. Well educated, of good address, and with a quiet, gentlemanly air about him that induced a favorable opinion at a glance. Frequently, prior to this, occasions had presented themselves for testing his abilities, and I had always found him equal to any emergency. Sagacious and skillful as I knew him to be, I felt that I could implicitly rely upon him to glean all the information that was required in order to enable me to devise an intelligent plan of detection, and which would, as I hoped, lead to eventual success.

Giving John Manning full instructions as to his mode of proceeding, and cautioning him to be particular and thorough in all his inquiries, I directed him to proceed as soon as possible to the scene of the robbery, and enter at once upon the performance of his duties.

In a very short time Manning had made his preparations, and at eight o'clock that evening he was at the depot awaiting the departure of the train that was to bear him to his new field of operation.

After a journey of several hours, in which the detective endeavored to snatch as much comfort as possible, the train drew up at the neat little station at Geneva, and Manning was upon the ground.

It was two o'clock in the morning when he arrived, consequently there were but few people stirring, and the station was almost entirely deserted. Two or three passengers who were awaiting the train, the persons connected with the railroad, and the runners of the two hotels (Geneva boasted of two of these very necessary establishments), were the only persons who greeted him upon his arrival.

Having never been to Geneva before, and being entirely ignorant of the accommodations afforded by either of these houses of entertainment, Manning, at a hazard, selected the "Geneva Hotel" as his place of abode. Consigning his valise to the care of the waiting porter, he was soon on his way to that hostelry, and serenely journeyed along through the darkness, all unconscious of the reception that awaited him. On arriving at their destination, he perceived through the glimmering light that hung over the doorway, that the "Geneva Hotel" was an old, rambling frame structure, which stood in the midst of an overgrowth of bushes and shrubbery. So dense was the foliage that the detective imagined the air of the place was damp and unwholesome in consequence. Certain it was, as he discovered afterward, the air and sunshine had a desperate struggle almost daily to obtain an entrance into the building, and after a few hours engaged in the vain attempt, old Sol would vent his baffled rage upon the worm-eaten old roof, to the decided discomfort of the lodgers in the attic story.

Ceremony was an unheard-of quality at the "Geneva House," and the railway porter performed the multifarious duties of night clerk, porter, hall boy and hostler. As they entered the hotel, the porter lighted a small lamp with the aid of a stable lantern, and without further parley led the detective up two flights of stairs which cracked and groaned under their feet, as if complaining of their weight, and threatening to precipitate them to the regions below. Opening the door of a little box of a room, out of which the hot air came rushing like a blast from a furnace fire, the porter placed the lamp upon a dilapidated wash-stand and the valise upon the floor, and without uttering a word, took himself off.

With all its progressiveness, it was evident that Geneva was far behind the age in regard to her hotel accommodations; at least so thought Manning as he gazed disconsolately around upon his surroundings. The room was small, close and hot, while the furniture exceeded his powers of description. The unpainted wash-stand seemed to poise itself uneasily upon its three remaining legs — the mirror had evidently been the resort of an army of self-admiring flies, who had left their marks upon its leaden surface until reflection was impossible — two hard and uncomfortable-looking chairs — and a bed, every feature of which was a sonorous protest against being slept upon — completed the provisions which had been made for his entertainment and comfort. Casting a dismal look upon his uninviting quarters, but being thoroughly tired, the detective threw himself upon the couch, which rattled and creaked under him like old bones, and in a few moments was sound asleep.

How long he might have remained in this somnolent condition if left to himself, it is impossible to state, for a vigorous alarm upon his door cut short his slumbers, and startled him from his dreams.

Imagining that the hotel had taken fire, or that the porter had eloped with the silverware, he jumped hastily out of bed and opened the door.

"It's late and breakfast is waitin'," was the laconic message delivered to him by the porter of the night before, as he started away.

With a muttered malediction upon this ruthless destroyer of his rest, the detective donned his clothing, and, feeling as tired and unrefreshed as though he had not slept at all, descended to the dining room. If his experiences of the previous evening had been distressing, the breakfast which was set before him was positively heart-rending. A muddy-looking liquid which they called coffee — strong, soggy biscuits, a beefsteak that would rival in toughness a piece of baked gutta percha, and evidently swimming in lard, and potatoes which gave decided tokens of having been served on more than one previous occasion. With a smothered groan he attacked the unsavory viands, and by dint of great effort managed to appease his hunger, to the serious derangement of his digestive organs. After he had finished his repast he lighted a cigar, and as the hour was still too early for a conference with the bank officials, he resolved to stroll about the town and ascertain the locality of the Geneva bank, before entering upon the duties of the investigation.

His stroll, however, was not a very extended one, for as he started from the hotel he noticed upon the opposite side of the street the sign of the bank. The building in which it was located was a large, square brick structure, occupied in part by the bank, and in part as a store for the sale of hardware and agricultural implements. The upper floor was used as an amusement hall, and was called the "Geneva Opera House." Here the various entertainments of a musical and dramatic nature were given, to the intense delight of the people of the village.

There was no notice of the bank having suspended operations on account of the loss they had sustained, and the operative inferred from this, that business was being transacted as usual.

When the doors were at length opened the operative entered the banking room, and requesting to see Mr. Silby, was ushered into the private office of the president. As he passed through the room he took a passing inventory of the young assistant cashier, Mr. Pearson, who was busily engaged upon his books. He appeared to be a young man of about twenty-four years of age; of a delicate and refined cast of countenance and about medium height. His hair and a small curly mustache were of a light brown shade, and his complexion was as fair as a woman's. The young lady who had been the other victim of the assault was not present, and the detective concluded that she was as yet unable to attend to her duties.

These thoughts and impressions passed through his mind as he walked through the banking room into the office of the president. As he entered this apartment, he found several gentlemen evidently await-ing his appearance, all of whom wore a thoughtful, troubled look, as though they keenly felt the losses they had sustained and were resolved to bear up manfully under their misfortune.

Mr. Silby, the president, a tall, fine-looking gentleman in the prime of life, arose as the detective entered. Mr. Silby was one of those persons who instinctively impress the beholder, with a confidence closely ap-proaching to veneration. Of a commanding presence, a broad noble face surmounted with a wealth of hair in which the silvery touch of time has left many traces, while his deep blue eyes were as bright as those of a youth of twenty. There was such an air of rugged and uncompromising honesty, of kindly feeling and warm-heartedness about the man, that even before he had spoken the detective experienced a strong impulse of regard for him, and a corresponding determination to perform his full duty in this investigation and to devote all the energy of his being to the task before him.

Presenting his letter of introduction, Mr. Silby hastily ran his eyes over the contents, and then extending his hand he gave the detective a most cordial greeting, and introduced him to the other gentlemen present, all of whom received him warmly.

"Take a seat, Mr. Manning," said Mr. Silby, drawing up a chair. "You find us anxiously awaiting your arrival, and prepared to give you any information you desire."

"Thanks," responded the operative, taking the proffered chair. "As I have come here for the purpose of making an examination into this case, I shall require all the information that is possible to obtain."

"Very well," said Mr. Silby. "Now, what do you desire first?"

"A full statement as to how the robbery was committed," answered the detective, promptly.

"Mr. Welton," said Mr. Silby, turning to a gentleman at his right, who had been introduced to the detective as the cashier of the bank, "perhaps you can relate the particulars better than I can."

"Excuse me," interrupted the detective, "but were you present at the time the robbery occurred?"

"No, sir, I was not present," replied Mr. Welton. "Mr. Pearson, our assistant cashier, and Miss Patton, were the only persons in the bank at that time."

"Then," said the detective, "suppose we have Mr. Pearson in at once, and hear the story from him. We always prefer," he added, with a smile, "to receive the particulars of these affairs from eyewitnesses."

The other gentlemen nodded a cordial assent to this proposition, and Mr. Welton arose, and going to the door, requested Mr. Pearson to enter the consulting room.

The young man entered the office, and upon being introduced, greeted the detective with an air of frank earnestness, and signified his readiness to relate all that he knew about the robbery.

He remained standing, and from his statement the facts were elicited which I have given in the preceding chapter. As he finished, he pointed to a scar upon his forehead, which he stated was the result of the blow he received at the time from the robber who attacked him. The wound did not appear to be a very serious one, although the skin had been broken and blood had evidently flowed freely.

"Mr. Pearson," inquired the detective, after the young man had concluded, "do you remember having seen either of those men before?"

The assistant cashier darted a quick glance at the detective, and then answered:

"Yes, sir; about three o'clock yesterday afternoon, a well-dressed gentleman came into the bank, carrying a small valise in his hand, which he requested permission to leave here until the next morning. I asked him if it was of any value, and he replied no. Informing him that I would then place it in the office, the man thanked me, and went away. When the two men entered the bank at six o'clock in the evening, I instantly recognized one of them as the man who had called in the afternoon. He was, however, dressed very roughly on the occasion of this last visit, and had evidently changed his clothes for the purpose of escaping detection or recognition."

"Which one of the men attacked you?" now asked the detective.

"The one who left the valise in the afternoon. While the tallest of the two was struggling with Miss Patton, who was screaming loudly, the other one came behind the counter and struck me upon the head with the butt end of his revolver. I became insensible after this, and knew nothing until I found myself in the vault."

"How did you extricate yourself from this dilemma?" inquired Manning.

"Well, sir," began Pearson; and the detective imagined that he noticed a hesitancy in his manner, which was not apparent before, "when I recovered consciousness, I found myself locked up in the vault, with Miss Patton lying beside me. When she recovered, we both shouted loudly for help, and beat with our hands upon the iron doors, in the hope of attracting attention. This failed, and we were nearly desperate. Just then, however, my foot came in contact with some loose silver upon the floor, and on stooping to pick them up, I found that they were ten-cent pieces. Instantly, the idea occurred to me, to attempt to remove the screws which fastened the lock to the inside of the door, and of using one of these coins for the purpose. To my intense joy the screws yielded to my efforts, and in a short time the heavy door swung open, and we were free. I have told you already what followed."

As John Manning jotted these recitals down in his notebook, he could not repress nor account for, a feeling of doubtfulness which crept over him at this point. He looked up into the young man's face, but there he saw only the evidence of serious truthfulness, and honest frankness; but still that lingering doubt was upon him and he could not shake it off.

At his request, young Pearson then furnished him with a description of the two men, as nearly as his memory would serve him, and these the detective noted down for future use.

At length, finding that he had obtained all the information which could be afforded him here, he thanked the gentlemen for their assistance, and promised to call again in the course of the day.

"Remember, Mr. Manning," said Mr. Silby, "we rely entirely upon the resources of Mr. Pinkerton's agency, and that we are confident that you will succeed."

"I cannot promise that," returned Manning, "but you may be assured that if success is possible, we will accomplish it."

So saying, he shook hands with the gentlemen, and left the bank. He betook himself at once to the hotel to prepare himself for further action in this investigation.

Chapter III

An Interview with Miss Patton — Important Revelations — Doubts Strengthened — Mr. Bartman's Story — William Resolves to Seek Newton Edwards.

*A*s the morning was not yet very far advanced, John Manning concluded to pay a visit to Miss Patton, the other eyewitness to, and active participant in the robbery.

Ascertaining the locality of her residence, he walked along the pleasant shaded street, revolving in his mind the various points upon which he had been enlightened during the interview just concluded. Arriving at his destination, he found a neat, cozy little cottage, set in the midst of a bright garden of blooming flowers, the perfume of which filled the morning air. There was an appearance of neatness and beauty and comfort about the place, which at once gave evidence of the refinement of those who dwelt within, and as the detective walked along the graveled path that led to the front door, he found himself involuntarily arranging his shirt-collar, and calling up his best manner for the occasion.

His knock was responded to by a kindly-faced, matronly looking lady, whom he instinctively felt was the mother of the young lady. Making his business known, and requesting an interview with Miss Patton, he was ushered into a cool, well-furnished parlor, to await the conveyance of his message and to learn the disposition of the invalid.

In a few minutes the lady reappeared, and stated that although her daughter was still very weak and nervous from the shock she had sustained, she would see him, and requested him to step into her room.

Entering a neatly furnished little chamber, he beheld the young lady reclining upon a couch, looking very pale, but with a pleasant smile of welcome upon her face that at once gave him the courage to proceed with the unpleasant business he had in hand.

Bidding her a polite good morning, he took the seat, which had been placed for him near the bed, and as delicately as possible, stated his business and the reason for his calling upon her. At this point Mrs. Patton excused herself, and retired, with the evident intention of leaving them alone.

Manning quietly and delicately made his inquiries, and the girl answered them in a plain, straightforward manner. Her story corroborated all that had previously been related by young Pearson, and left no doubt in the mind of the detective that the occurrences of the eventful afternoon had been correctly detailed. He could not, however, control the doubtfulness that was impressing him with regard to Eugene Pearson.

"I cannot forbear the thought," said he, when Miss Patton had concluded her story, "that if Mr. Pearson had displayed a reasonable amount of manly bravery, this robbery could not have taken place."

"There is something very strange to me," said the girl, musingly, "about the manner in which Eugene acted; and — there are some things that I cannot understand."

"Would you object to telling me what they are?" said the detective. "Perhaps I can enlighten you."

"Well," responded the girl reluctantly, "I fear that Eugene has not told the entire truth in this matter."

"In what respect?" inquired the detective.

"I would not do anything to injure Mr. Pearson for the world, Mr. Manning, and he may have forgotten the circumstance altogether, but I am sure that I saw one of those robbers on two occasions before this occurred, in the bank and talking to Mr. Pearson."

"Why should he seek to conceal this?" asked the operative.

"That is just what I cannot understand," answered the lady.

"Tell me just what you know, and perhaps I can help you in coming to a correct conclusion."

"I don't like to say anything about this, but still I think it is my duty to do so, and I will tell you all that I know. More than two weeks ago, I returned from my dinner to the bank one day, and I saw this man in the private office with Mr. Pearson; I noticed then that their manner toward each other showed them to be old acquaintances rather than mere strangers. This man left the bank in a few minutes after I came in. He had the manner and appearance of a gentleman, and I did not think anything of it at the time."

"Did Mr. Pearson tell you who he was, or explain his presence there at that time?"

"No, I did not ask anything about him, and he did not mention the matter to me."

"When did you see them together again?"

"That same evening about dusk. I had been making a call upon a friend, and was returning home when I met them walking and conversing together."

"Did Mr. Pearson recognize you on that occasion?" inquired the detective.

"No, sir, he did not seem to notice me at all, and I passed them without speaking."

"You are quite sure about this?"

"Oh, yes, quite sure. I recognized him immediately when he came yesterday afternoon to leave the valise in the bank, and also when he came with the other man when the robbery was committed."

"Do you feel confident that you would be able to identify him, if you were to see him again?"

"I am quite sure that I would," returned the girl confidently, "his features are too indelibly fixed in my mind for me to make any mistake about it."

"Have you said anything to Mr. Pearson about this?"

"Yes; as soon as we were out of the vault, I said to him – 'One of those men was the man who left the valise and the same one I saw in the office the other day.'"

"What reply did he make."

"He appeared to be doubtful, and simply said, 'Is that so?'"

"Very well, Miss Patton," said the detective at length, "we will look fully into this matter; but in the meantime, I particularly desire that you will say nothing to anyone about what you have told me today. It is very necessary that a strict silence should be preserved upon this point."

The young lady cheerfully promised compliance with this request, and in a few moments the detective, after thanking her for her kindness in seeing him, arose and took his departure.

As he strolled back to the hotel, he revolved the information he had received carefully in his mind. He had also obtained from Miss Patton a description of the two men, and found that they agreed very nearly with what he had learned from Mr. Pearson. He went to his room immediately, and prepared a report of all that had transpired during the morning, carefully detailing all that he had heard relating to Mr. Pearson's alleged intimacy with one of the robbers, and of the successful attempt he made to extricate himself from the vault, by means of the ten-cent piece. After concluding his relations, he requested the assistance of another operative, in order that they might scour the country round about, in the hope of finding some clues of the escaping robbers.

On the next morning, operative Howard Jackson, a young, active and extremely intelligent member of my force, arrived at Geneva, and placed himself in communication with John Manning, for the continuance of this investigation.

When Manning's reports were duly received by my son, William A. Pinkerton, the superintendent of my Chicago agency, he gave the matter his most careful and earnest attention, and as he finished their perusal, he formed the opinion that young Pearson was not entirely guiltless of some collusion in this robbery. The more he weighed the various circumstances connected with this case, the more firm did this conclusion become, until at last he experienced a firm conviction that this young man knew more about the matter than he had yet related.

It seemed strange to him that a young, strong and active man like Pearson should not have manifested even ordinary courage in a crisis like this. He was behind the desk when the attack was made upon Miss Patton at the door, and saw what was transpiring before the second assailant had time to reach him. Even if powerless to defend her, it seemed reasonable that he could have raised an alarm, which would have attracted the attention of the passers by; or, failing in that, he could, at least, have hastily closed the vault doors, and thus have saved the money of the bank. He knew that these doors were open, and that within the vault were nearly thirty thousand dollars, for which he was indirectly responsible. But a moment's time would have sufficed to close these doors and adjust the combination, and yet he made no effort to prevent a robbery which he knew was intended.

The ordinary promptings of manhood would, it was thought, have induced him to make some show of resistance, or to have gone to the rescue of a young and delicate girl; but none of these things did he do, and, if the story related was true, the young man had acted like a base coward at the best, and submitted without a murmur to the outrages that were perpetrated in his presence. Instead of acting like a man, he stood tamely by and allowed a woman to be cruelly beaten, the bank robbed, and the robbers to walk off unmolested and unharmed.

There was another matter which seemed impossible of accomplishment. Pearson had stated that while in the vault he had removed the screws from the lock upon the door with the aid of a ten-cent piece. This idea seemed to be utterly incredible, and prompted by his doubts, William attempted the same feat upon the lock on his office door. After several efforts, in which he exerted his strength to the utmost, he was obliged to desist. The screws utterly defied the efforts to move them, while the coin was bent and twisted out of all shape, by the pressure that it was subjected to.

While he was thus engaged with his thoughts upon this perplexing problem, he was informed that two gentlemen from Geneva desired to speak with him. Signifying his readiness to receive them, two well-dressed gentlemen entered and announced their business.

One of these men was a Mr. Perry, a director of the Geneva bank, and his companion was a Mr. Bartman, a merchant in Newtonsville, a little town situated but a few miles distant from Geneva.

"Mr. Bartman," said Mr. Perry, addressing my son, "has some information to communicate, which I think is important enough to deserve serious consideration, and I have brought him to you."

Mr. Bartman's information proved to be of very decided importance. He stated that he was a merchant, doing business in Newtonsville, and that he was in the habit of purchasing his goods from various traveling salesmen who represented Chicago houses. Among this number was a young man named Newton Edwards, who was in the employ of a large commission house, located on South Water Street, in the city of Chicago. He had known Edwards for some years, and had frequently dealt with him during that period. During the forenoon of the day on which the robbery occurred, he saw Newton Edwards in Newtonsville, but that instead of attempting to sell his goods, that gentleman was apparently seeking to avoid observation. He met him upon the street and familiarly accosted him, but Edwards received his salutations coldly, and did not engage in any conversation. Mr. Bartman thought nothing of this at the time, but in the afternoon, having business in Geneva, he drove over to that place, and, to his surprise, he found Edwards, in company with a strange young man, lingering around the public house in Geneva, apparently having nothing whatever to do. He noticed also, that Edwards was somewhat under the influence of liquor, and that he had effected a complete change in his apparel. A few hours after this he heard of the robbery, and instantly his mind reverted to the strange appearance and actions of Newton Edwards. He endeavored to find him, but, as if in confirmation of his suspicions, both Edwards and his companion had disappeared.

Mr. Bartman gave a full description of Edwards as he appeared that day; and in substantiation of his suspicions, it was found to agree perfectly with that given by both Eugene Pearson and Miss Grace Patton.

Mr. Perry stated that within two hours after the robbery had been discovered, men had been sent out in all directions, in search of the fleeing robbers, but without success. They had only been enabled to learn that two men, carrying a valise between them, had been seen walking along the railroad track in a northwesterly direction from Geneva, but that was all. In the darkness of the night, they had succeeded in eluding their pursuers, and on the following day all traces of them were obscured.

Two things were now to be done at once; to ascertain the antecedents of Eugene Pearson, and to seek the whereabouts of Newton Edwards. To these tasks William applied himself immediately, and with what result will be shown hereafter.

Chapter IV

The work progresses — Eugene Pearson's early life — On the trail of Newton Edwards.

In the meantime operatives Manning and Jackson had been untiring in their efforts to obtain some traces of the robbers. They had found a number of people who recollected seeing two men, answering the description of the suspected thieves, who carried a valise between them, but beyond a certain point all traces of them stopped. It seemed that the ground had opened and swallowed them up, so effectual had been their disappearance.

While thus engaged, operative Manning received instructions to keep a watchful eye upon young Pearson, and also to make quiet and judicious inquiries as to his habits and associates in Geneva.

The result of these inquiries was most favorable to the young man, and under ordinary circumstances would have disarmed suspicion at once. During the progress of this search after truth, operative Manning had preserved the utmost good feeling and cordiality in his dealings with Eugene Pearson, and had succeeded in establishing a friendly intimacy with him, that would have allayed any fears which the young man might have had, as to the opinions entertained by the detectives with regard to himself. Mr. Pearson was very positive that one of the robbers was the same man who had left the valise at the bank during the afternoon, and, after learning that Manning had paid a visit to Miss Patton, he stated his belief that this same person had called at the bank a few weeks before. He could not remember the name he had given at that time, but thought he had inquired as to the financial standing of several of the business men of Geneva. During all these interviews Mr. Pearson displayed the utmost willingness to assist the detectives in their investigation, and with a frankness that was refreshing, answered every question that was put to him as if with the earnest desire of facilitating their labors and contributing to the accomplishment of their success.

Eugene Pearson was a young man, it was learned, who had first seen the light in the little town of Geneva, then a straggling little village with none of the pretensions it now presented. His parents were most exemplary people, and his father at one time had been a wealthy grain merchant, but during one of the financial panics that swept over the country, he was unfortunate enough to suffer embarrassments which stripped him of his fortune and left him penniless in his old age to begin again the battle of life. At the present time, he was a benevolent-looking, intelligent old gentleman, who occupied the honorable and not very lucrative position of postmaster of Geneva, from the receipts of which, and a few other interests he was enabled to maintain his family in comparative comfort.

Young Pearson had grown to manhood surrounded by the refining influences of his family, and, save for a few months spent at a business college in a neighboring city, had always dwelt in his native town. Among the residents of Geneva he was universally respected and admired. Possessed, as he was, of more than ordinary intelligence, and evincing good business qualifications, he had occupied his present position in the bank for several years, and at the time of the robbery, arrangements were being made for his promotion to the position of cashier, owing to the contemplated retirement of Mr. Welton, the present incumbent. His personal habits were unexceptionable, so far as known, and everyone with whom John Manning conversed upon the subject, were loud in his praises. In the social circles of the town, he was an acknowledged favorite; he was a fair musician, was a member of the choir in the leading church of Geneva, and a teacher in the Sunday-school. His handsome face and pleasing manners gained for him a host of friends, and his companionship was eagerly sought by the young people with whom he associated. The young ladies were particularly partial to his society, and it was stated that he was engaged to be married to a beautiful young lady of the town, whose father was one of the wealthiest men in the country round about. At the bank, he was held in high esteem by both the officers and directors, and Mr. Silby's affection for him amounted almost to the love of a father for a favorite child. From infancy to manhood his name had never been associated with aught that was injurious or degrading, and among all the young men of Geneva, Eugene Pearson stood highest in public esteem and general favor.

The result of these inquiries were not calculated to strengthen the doubts which had been formed of young Pearson's participation in this robbery, and yet the suspicion remained unchanged, and we determined to await developments before yielding our opinions to what seemed to be a pressure of circumstances.

In the meantime, William had not been idle in the city. Ascertaining the name of the firm for which Newton Edwards was traveling, and determined to satisfy his mind upon this point, he dispatched an operative to the business house to which he had been referred. The result of this inquiry was that Mowbray, Morton & Co., the firm with which Edwards had at one time been engaged, stated that he had severed his connection with them a short time before, and since then had done nothing for them, but had been traveling for another house on the same street, and they believed he was the junior partner of the firm. Inquiry at this house elicited the information that Edwards had retired from this firm, and had connected himself with a large eastern house, which dealt extensively in fruits and a general line of groceries. At this place, however, several items of information were gleaned which were of importance. The gentlemen connected with this establishment were very well acquainted with Newton Edwards, of whom they spoke in the highest terms. He had been in Chicago during all of the week previous to the robbery, but had left the city on Saturday, stating that he intended to travel through Wisconsin and Minnesota in the interest of the new firm which he represented. He had not been seen since, nor had they heard from him.

Finding that the gentleman who furnished this information was an intimate acquaintance of Edwards, the operative next inquired as to his family connections and his place of residence. On these points he was fully informed, and he cheerfully imparted the desired information. Edwards, it appeared, had been married recently to a lovely and accomplished young lady from one of the outlying towns, and since his marriage had been residing with the husband of his sister, a gentleman named Samuel Andrews, who resided at 29 Logan Place, in Chicago. Edwards also had a brother who was married, and who lived in the city, and the location of this gentleman's residence was also cheerfully furnished by the merchant.

Upon returning with this information, the operative at once reported to my son William, who decided upon an immediate course of action. Directing the operative to inquire for tidings of Edwards at both of the places named, he indited a telegraphic message to the chief of police at Milwaukee and Minneapolis, for the purpose of ascertaining if Edwards had been at either place since leaving the city. He described the man fully, stated the name of the house which he represented, gave the fullest particulars as to his identity, and then requested to be informed if he had made his appearance in either of these cities.

To all these messages the answer was received that Edwards had not, as yet, arrived, although the chief at Milwaukee stated that he had met a friend of Edwards, who informed him that he had received a letter from the young man dated four days prior to the robbery, stating that he would be in Milwaukee in a few days, and that he would be accompanied by his wife. As yet, however, he had not arrived, and nothing further had been heard of him.

This was a corroboration of the first suspicion regarding Newton Edwards, and was convincing of the fact that he had not done as he had informed his friends that he would do. William was convinced, therefore, that he was upon the right track, and impatiently awaited the return of the operative who had been sent to the residences of Edwards' relatives.

The detective delegated for that purpose proceeded to the locality to which he had been directed, where he found a comfortable-looking, well-kept brick dwelling-house, and upon a metal plate upon the door, he noticed the name he was in search of. Ascending the steps, he rang the bell, and shortly afterward was ushered into a handsomely furnished parlor, where he was greeted by a pleasant-faced lady, who announced herself as the sister of Mr. Newton Edwards.

"Is Mr. Edwards residing with you?" inquired the detective.

"Not now," answered the lady, "he was here until Saturday last, when he left, saying that he was going to Milwaukee upon business. I have heard however, that he was in town on Sunday last, but that I am not sure of."

"Did his wife go with him?" now asked the operative, hoping to obtain an interview with her, if possible.

"No, sir," replied Mrs. Andrews, with an air of sudden coldness and reserve, which was not lost upon the watchful man before her. "Mrs. Edwards left on the same day, in company with her brother, who has taken her to his home; I do not wish to allude to this matter, but I am afraid my brother and his wife do not live happily together."

"Have they separated?" asked the detective, in a tone of solicitude.

After a momentary hesitation, the woman replied: "I am inclined to think they have. Newton has not been himself lately, and has, I am sorry to say, been drinking a great deal. This naturally led to harsh treatment of his wife, and I presume she wrote to her brother, and on last Saturday he came and took her away."

Finding the lady indisposed to furnish further information, the detective took his leave.

At the second place he received much the same information, and concluding that he had exhausted this matter, he started to return to the agency. At this latter place, however, he had casually inquired for the name and residence of Mrs. Edwards' brother, and on learning that, had concluded his visit.

Everything thus far had favored a belief that Edwards was concerned in this robbery. His leaving home a day or two before the act was committed, his quarrel with his wife, his statement made to friends that he was going upon a business trip, which it was evident he had not done, his strange appearance at Newtonsville and Geneva on the day the robbery took place, the fact that his personal appearance agreed perfectly with that given of the robber, by eyewitnesses to that event, and his mysterious disappearance since, all went to prove beyond question that Newton Edwards was the thief, and that decided steps should be taken to discover his whereabouts.

Leaving William to devise a plan to accomplish this much-desired result, we will return to Geneva, and watch the movements of John Manning and Howard Jackson.

Chapter V

New developments — Tidings of Newton Edwards — Suspicions strengthening against Eugene Pearson — Mr. Silby's confidence.

*I*n extending their investigations in and around Geneva, operatives Manning and Jackson had discovered numerous items of intelligence corroborative of their previous suspicions. A salesman, connected with a large mercantile house from one of the large cities, furnished the information that on Monday, the day on which the robbery occurred, he had traveled with Edwards as far as Newtonsville, and as he did not see him after leaving that place, he concluded that he must have stopped there. He also stated that Edwards appeared to be unusually cold and reserved, and that he was accompanied by a companion whom he did not introduce to his friends. At Newtonsville it was learned that a man, fully answering the description of Edwards' companion, had visited both of the livery stables in that town, and had attempted to hire a team of horses and a carriage. He had been refused in both instances, for the reasons that he was a stranger, and appeared to be under the influence of liquor. Several people both in Geneva and Newtonsville were found who remembered seeing Edwards, whom they knew — and a companion who was a stranger to them — about these towns on the day of the robbery, and they described their actions as being very peculiar. They had disappeared immediately after that and had not been seen since. If further proofs of the complicity of Edwards were required they could have been procured by the score, and as all traces of their route from Geneva had been lost, William resolved to commence a thorough and systematic process of espionage, which he believed would eventually lead to the discovery of his hiding place. He thoroughly canvassed the situation and his conclusions were soon found. Newton Edwards had a father and mother — he had brothers and sisters; and in addition to these he had a lovely young wife, from whom he had parted in anger. It was not possible that he could shake himself loose from all these ties of kindred and affection at one blow, and it was reasonably sure that sooner or later he would attempt to correspond with them in some manner. Again, it might be the case that some of his relatives were already aware of his crime, and of the fact that he was hiding from the officers of the law, and it could not be expected that they would voluntarily give information that would lead to his discovery. However grieved and disappointed they might be, however angry they must naturally feel, they could not be expected at such a time as this to turn his accusers, and aid in his capture.

I have known cases in the course of my professional practice, however, when fathers, actuated by what they considered the highest motives, have delivered up their sons to the law, and, though the ordeal was an exceedingly trying and distressing one, they never faltered for a moment in what they considered the performance of their duty. I need not say that such evidences of self-sacrifice were painful to me, and that my feelings were always deeply touched by the mental sufferings of the poor criminals, who in the hour of their sorest need, found themselves deserted by the only friends upon whom they believed they could rely in an emergency which threatened disgrace and servitude.

While this is true, it is equally certain that I have yet to record a single case in which a female relative ever assisted, in any manner, toward the apprehension of a criminal. No power seemed able to force from her a word that would tend to work him injury, and though her heart was breaking, and her love for the lost one had passed away, yet, with a persistence worthy of all admiration, she refused to do aught that would add to the misery of the fallen one; and, if occasion offered, invariably rendered her assistance to secure his escape.

Taking these ideas into consideration, therefore, it would not do to rely at all upon any assistance from the relatives of Edwards, and to advise them of our suspicions and search, would naturally only tend to place both him and them upon their guard.

A slower and more laborious operation was therefore necessary. Fully in earnest in his determination to capture these men, and firmly supported by the officials of the bank, who were as resolute as he in their resolve to apprehend the robbers, William at once put this plan into execution.

Operatives were posted to watch the residences of the relatives of Edwards in the city, and instructed to carefully note their actions, particularly in the matter of receiving or posting of any letters. Another operative was dispatched to Woodford to note the movements of Mrs. Edwards, the wife of the suspected thief, and to endeavor to obtain some information that would assist us in the chase. It might be possible that this reported quarrel was a mere ruse, to blind the detectives, and to throw them off the scent; and it was important that the truthfulness of this story should be substantiated. At the same time, William decided on no account to lose sight of young Pearson, and directed the operatives at Geneva to maintain a strict watch over his movements, and by no means to permit him to leave town unaccompanied by someone who could note his every action. The young bank clerk, however, gave no cause for any new suspicion. He performed his duties at the bank with unflagging industry and evinced the greatest desire that the thieves might soon be captured. His solicitude for Miss Patton was apparently sincere and unceasing, and he frequently reproached himself for not having acted in a more manly manner at the time the assault was made. So humiliated did he appear at the loss the bank had sustained, and so earnest was he in everything that approached a vigorous and determined chase after the robbers, that he soon became an object of profound sympathy and higher regard to the bank officers and his numerous friends in Geneva. After fully considering this matter of young Pearson, William deemed it his duty to acquaint Mr. Silby with his suspicions. It was due to that gentleman, he argued, that he should be thus informed, and then if results should justify the suspicion he would be prepared for what would follow, while if the contrary should prove true he would have all the more reason for his high estimation of his young assistant cashier.

He did not have long to wait before making this revelation, for in a few days after he had put his plans into operation and posted his men, William received a call from Mr. Silby, who desired to be informed of the progress that was being made. After fully detailing to the honest old banker all that we had thus far learned, and the steps which had been taken to ascertain the whereabouts of Newton Edwards, all of which met with his hearty approval, William delicately broached the unpleasant subject.

"Mr. Silby," said he, "there is another matter which I desire to speak of, and one which I fear may occasion you some pain, or may meet with your opposition."

"Let me know what it is, by all means," responded Mr. Silby, with a smile. "I am satisfied that what you have to say is for the best interests of the bank, and it would be absurd in me to offer opposition to that."

"Well," said William, "there have been certain developments made in this case which, I regret to say, lead me to believe that Eugene Pearson is not entirely blameless in this robbery."

"What do you mean?" exclaimed Mr. Silby, starting to his feet, and with a tremor in his voice, which told of inward agitation; "you do not mean that you suspect Eugene?"

"I must confess that I do," said William solemnly, "and I regret it sincerely, both on your account and his own."

"But this will not do," suddenly interrupted the old gentleman, "this cannot be. Why, I have known that boy ever since his childhood, and I have loved him as my own son. No, no, Mr. Pinkerton, you must be mistaken about this."

"Mr. Silby," said my son, "let us look at this matter calmly and dispassionately. You have employed us to ferret out the thieves, and to recover, if possible, the money of which you have been robbed. We have therefore but one duty to perform, and that is to find the men. I have looked into this case carefully; I have noted every point thus far attained; I have weighed every item philosophically, and I tell you now, that I am convinced that Eugene Pearson knows more about this robbery than has yet been revealed."

William then slowly and concisely detailed the various points upon which he founded his suspicions. The fact that Eugene Pearson had been seen in intimate conversation with the suspected man, his presence at the bank on the afternoon of the robbery, his actions, cowardly at best, when the assault was made upon the helpless girl, his peculiar statements since, and then the manner of his release by the aid of the ten-cent silver piece. Taking a coin from his pocket, he requested Mr. Silby to attempt the feat upon the slight lock upon the office door, which he tried, and though he labored strenuously, he was unable to move it. He also informed him that Manning had attempted the same thing upon the lock of the vault door, and that he could not budge a screw. All these facts he pointed out to the old gentleman as strong proofs of the young man's guilt.

Mr. Silby sat during this recital with a dazed and stricken look upon his face, and when William had finished, he sat for a time in speechless amazement. Recovering himself at length, he said:

"Mr. Pinkerton, this may all prove to be true; but at present, you must excuse me, I cannot believe it — it is too terrible."

True and trustful old man! he could not be brought to believe that one so dearly loved and highly trusted could prove so base and undeserving.

"Now, Mr. Silby," said William, "I have only this to ask — I may be wrong, or I may be right; but until definite results are achieved, I must request you to keep this matter a profound secret, and to keep a close watch upon young Pearson without exciting his suspicion; will you do this?"

"I will do what you request," responded Mr. Silby; "but believe me, you will find that you are mistaken."

"Another thing," continued William. "If at any time I should telegraph to you these words — *'Look out for that package!'* please remember that 'that package' means Pearson, and he must not be allowed to go away."

"All this I will do, because I know you are doing what you think best; but I am confident all will be made right for the boy in good time."

"For your sake, Mr. Silby, I hope so, too, but I am not so sanguine of that: and we cannot afford to take any risks."

Mr. Silby arose to his feet, and grasping my son's hand, withdrew without a word. As he passed out, William looked after him with a feeling of compassion he rarely experienced.

"It is a great pity," he murmured to himself, "that so much strong, manly faith should be so sadly misplaced, and I fear very much that before we are through with this case, Mr. Silby's trust in human nature will be badly shattered. But we must do our duty, and the right must triumph at last — we must await the result."

Chapter VI

The Detective at Woodford. — An Interview with the Discarded Wife of Newton Edwards.

*I*t was on a hot sultry morning in August, about ten days after the robbery at Geneva, that William Everman arrived at the picturesque little city of Woodford. Woodford was the home of the brother of Mrs. Newton Edwards, with whom that lady was supposed to have taken refuge after her quarrel with her husband. Everman proceeded directly to the hotel upon his arrival, and quickly announced himself as a traveling salesman from a neighboring city. In a casual conversation with the clerk, he ascertained that Edwards and his wife were quite well known in the place, and that the clerk was an intimate acquaintance of the lady's husband.

"Is Edwards stopping here now?" inquired the detective, in a careless manner.

"No!" answered the clerk, as he fondly curled the ends of a very delicate and scarcely perceptible mustache. "He hasn't stopped here since his marriage; he usually goes to the home of his wife's family now."

"Do you know whether he is in town now?"

"I think not, unless he arrived last night," answered the young man. "There are several letters here for him, and he would have called for them before this. He has his mail always directed here."

"I am sorry for that," said Everman. "I have some instructions for him from the house he travels for, and he ought to get them as soon as possible."

"Perhaps Mr. Black could tell you where he is. I believe Edwards' wife is staying with him, and she certainly could tell you where you could address him, or whether he is expected here very soon."

After thanking the clerk for his information and ascertaining the business place of Mr. Black, the detective left the hotel, and sauntered about the city.

Walking leisurely down the main street, he soon came in sight of the place to which he had been directed. It was a small frame building, somewhat old and dilapidated, and was sadly in need of the painter's brush and a new covering of paint. Over the doorway swung a dingy, time-worn and weather-beaten sign, upon which he could barely decipher the words: "HENRY BLACK, Locksmith," and over which were suspended a pair of massive crossed keys which at one time had been bright golden, but which now were old and rusty looking. In the low window in front there was a rare and curious collection of articles that would have delighted the eyes of an antiquarian. Locks there were, that were relics of a bygone age, and seemed as if they might have done service on dungeon doors in some ancient keep in feudal times — strange and grotesque locks that had evidently pleased the fancy of some old connoisseur, whose treasures were guarded by these strange looking protectors, which had now outgrown their usefulness, and were exhibited as curiosities in the practical age of today. Locks of latest finish and design, and locks red and rusty and worn out, were mingled together with a confusion and carelessness that bespoke a thriving business, which left no time for order or arrangement.

Entering the shop without hesitation and with a careless air of assurance, Everman found himself in the presence of the locksmith, who was busily employed at his work. Mr. Black was a stout, good-looking, middle-aged man, who wore bushy whiskers and a pair of iron-rimmed spectacles. On the entrance of the detective he came forward with a pleasant smile on his face, as though expecting a profitable customer, and greeted the operative.

"Well, sir, what can I do for you today?"

"Nothing in the way of business," replied the detective; "I am seeking some information which perhaps you can give me."

"Take a seat," said the locksmith, pushing a stool toward the detective, and at the same time seating himself upon the counter. "I don't know a great deal, but if I can tell you what you want to know I shall be happy to do so."

"Thank you," replied Everman, as he produced a couple of fragrant cigars, and handed one to Mr. Black. "My name is Everman; I am a salesman for a city house, and am a neighbor of your brother-in-law, Newton Edwards. I have a message for him from his employer, and want to find out where to address him. I understood he had come to Woodford, and was informed at the hotel that I would be apt to learn from you whether he was in town."

While he was speaking, he watched the countenance of the locksmith carefully, and as he mentioned the name of Edwards he noticed that the cheerful smile disappeared from his face and was replaced with a heavy frown; this remained but a moment, and when Everman finished speaking, he promptly and pleasantly replied:

"I cannot tell you, I am sorry to say, where Mr. Edwards is at present, for I do not know myself. I only know that he was in Chicago on Saturday, a week ago, and at that time he stated that he was going to Milwaukee and St. Paul; whether he did so or not I cannot tell you."

"I understood from his employer that he and Mrs. Edwards contemplated stopping in Woodford for a few days before he started upon his business trip."

In response to this, Mr. Black stated to the detective, after much hesitation, but believing he was speaking to a friend, that on the Saturday mentioned, he had received a telegram from his sister, who was the wife of Newton Edwards, requesting him to come to her at once. He immediately responded to this summons, and on going to the house where she was stopping, he found her in great distress, and weeping violently. From her he then learned that Edwards had come to the house that morning in a state of intoxication, and had shamefully abused her. That he had ordered her to return to her family, and declared that he would never live with her again. Mr. Black had therefore brought his sister home with him, and threatened to inflict personal chastisement upon Edwards if he ever crossed his path again.

Finding that the story of the separation was a truthful one, at least so far as the relatives of Mrs. Edwards were concerned, Everman decided to obtain an interview, if possible, with the forsaken wife. Inviting Mr. Black to accompany him to the hotel, which was but a short distance from the shop, the locksmith took off his leather apron and paper cap, and the two strolled away together.

Over their cigars and a cooling draft of very good beer, the brother-in-law of the suspected criminal became quite friendly and communicative, relating many trifling particulars of Edwards' earlier life, which need not be repeated here. Preferring his request, at length, Mr. Black cordially invited him to his residence, and giving him explicit directions, suggested that he should call that afternoon. To this proposition Everman readily assented, and after a short time spent in friendly conversation, Mr. Black returned to his shop, and the detective wended his way to the locksmith's house.

Arriving at the place designated, he found a pretty little cottage, overgrown with climbing vines, while a garden of bright blooming flowers rendered the front of the house an attractive spot. Ascending the stoop, he rang the bell, and in a few moments a pleasant-faced lady appeared at the door. Inquiring if Mrs. Edwards was within, and being informed in the affirmative, he was invited to enter the cool and cozy parlor and await her appearance.

After a short delay Mrs. Edwards entered the room, and the heart of the detective was at once touched at the sad and sorrowful expression which she wore. She was young, scarcely more than twenty, and a handsome brunette. Her dark hair was brushed in wavy ringlets back from a broad, intellectual brow, and the dark eyes were dewy, as if with recent tears. Her cheeks were pale, and there were heavy shadows under the eyes, which told of sorrow and a heart ill at ease. Another thing the detective noticed, with a feeling of compassion, for he was himself a man of family, the lady was about to become a mother. How strange and unreasonable it seemed, that a young man of Edwards' position in society, with a lovely and loving wife, with business prospects of the most excellent character, could sacrifice all upon the altar of a base and ignoble ambition to be suddenly rich. That he could at one fell blow cast away the ties of kindred, the love of a devoted wife, the blissful anticipation of becoming a happy and proud father, and in an evil hour yield to a temptation which eventually would place the brand of the felon upon his brow, would cause him to be shunned and despised by his former friends and associates, clothe him in the garb of the convict, and, if justice were meted out to him, would make him an inmate of a prison. These thoughts flitted through the mind of the detective as he gazed upon the pale sad features of the suffering wife, and for a moment he regretted the profession which he had adopted. It is a common error,

I fear, to imagine that a detective is devoid of those finer feelings which animate humanity, and to credit him with only the hard, stern and uncompromising ideas of duty which only appear upon the surface. This is a grave mistake, and does gross injustice to many noble men and women, who, in my own experience, have developed some of the most delicate and noble traits of which human nature is capable. It is true, their duty is hard and unyielding, its imperative requirements must be rigidly observed; but many a criminal today has urgent reasons to be thankful to the man who was instrumental in bringing him to account for the crimes he had committed. Many a convict's wife and children are the recipients of kindly actions from the very men whose duty it was to deprive them, by a legal process, of a husband and father. This may seem strange and incredible, but from my own experience I can testify to its absolute truthfulness. With the capture of the criminal the detective's duty ceases, and all the sympathetic promptings of his nature have full play. He has performed his duty to the state, to the law and to society, and that done, his knowledge of the sufferings which crime have caused leads him to acts of kindness and of practical assistance. Today, I have some of the warmest and most grateful friends among the families of the men whom I was compelled to bring to justice, and in many cases the criminals themselves have acknowledged my actions, and have been better men in consequence. But this is a digression, and we will return to our narrative.

Rising to his feet, the detective politely acknowledged the salutation of Mrs. Edwards, and in as few words as possible he stated his errand. With painful embarrassment of manner, Mrs. Edwards informed him that she could not tell him anything about her husband's movements, as, contrary to his usual custom, he had not informed her of the route he intended to take when he left home. Not a word or a hint was given of the trouble that was preying upon her heart, of the harsh, unfeeling treatment to which she had been subjected, or of the brutal order, expulsion and separation. The dignity of the noble little woman sustained her grandly, and no confession of her wrongs escaped her lips. She then informed the detective that she expected to hear from him every day, and that she believed he was now traveling through Wisconsin.

That she was entirely unaware, at present at least, of her husband's whereabouts, the operative was firmly convinced; and she appeared to be equally uninformed of the suspicions that were entertained regarding him.

After a few moments spent in friendly converse, the detective arose to take his leave; and after being invited to renew his visit, he departed from the house.

"By George!" murmured Everman to himself, as he made his way back to the hotel; "that little woman is a wife to be proud of. That she knows nothing at present I am fully convinced, but I am also certain that if she learns of the crime her husband has committed, she would sacrifice her life rather than aid us in his discovery. What a strange, unequal world this is! — bad men linked with angelic wives; and vicious and unprincipled women yoked with men who are the very soul of honor. Well, well, I cannot set things right. I have only my duty to perform, and moralizing is very unprofitable."

So pondering he returned to the hotel and resolving to call upon the chief of police in the afternoon, he went into the spacious dining room and ordered his dinner.

Chapter VII

A Fire and a Talkative Fireman — Mrs. Edwards Receives a Letter.

*A*fter dinner operative Everman called upon the chief of police, and acquainting him fully with the nature of his business in the city, he enlisted his services in our behalf. Men were detailed to watch the arriving and departing trains, in order to discover if Edwards either paid a visit to Woodford or attempted to leave the place. This step was taken as a mere precaution, for the detective as yet felt confident that Mrs. Edwards was entirely ignorant of the movements of her husband or of the crime which he was suspected of committing. This was continued without result for three days, but on the afternoon of the fourth, the chief sought Everman at the hotel and informed him that he had important news to communicate.

"What is it?" inquired Everman, when they were alone.

"Well," said the chief, "it is just this. Last night, one of my men informs me, Mrs. Edwards received a letter from her husband, and today she appears to be in great trouble and distress of mind. There can be no doubt that she has been informed of his crime, and also that she now knows his present whereabouts."

"She will never tell anyone where that is, unless I am very much mistaken in her," interrupted Everman, "and we must look elsewhere for the information we desire."

"Just my opinion exactly," replied the chief; "and I have thought of a way in which we might get what we want."

"Let me hear what it is," said Everman.

"It is just this — Mrs. Black has an intimate friend and confidante, to whom she tells everything she knows, and there is no doubt that she will soon, if she has not already done so, inform this lady of the letter received yesterday. Well, so far, so good. Now, this lady has a husband to whom she tells all she hears, and so he is apt to be as well informed in a short time. This man is Tom Nelson by name, a carpenter by trade, and a jovial, easy, good-natured fellow by nature. This man you must work up, and if you touch him correctly, you will find out all he knows."

"Very good," replied Everman confidently; "now point out Tom Nelson to me and leave me to work the rest."

At this moment an alarm of fire was sounded, and in a few minutes the street in front of the hotel was alive with people hurrying to the scene of the conflagration. Men and boys were running at the top of their speed, and shouting at the top of their voices; women were gazing from doors and windows, and the merry jingle of the bells of the fire-engines were soon heard, as the brave fire laddies were rushing to the rescue of the burning building.

"The very thing!" ejaculated the chief. "I must go to the fire, and do you come along with me. Tom Nelson is one of the most active firemen of the city, and I will point him out to you. After that you must work your own way, for if I was to approach him upon the subject, he would become suspicious at once."

So saying the chief hurried out of the hotel, closely followed by the detective. Turning a corner they saw, not a great distance off, the flames leaping from the windows and roof of a large frame structure, which was blazing and crackling like a huge pile of kindling prepared for the torch. Already the department was upon the ground, and when the chief and the detective reached the scene, several streams of water, shimmering like ropes of silver, were pouring into the burning building. With a noble self-sacrifice and a disregard for their own safety which was truly admirable, the brave fire laddies battled with the flames, and exerted themselves to the utmost to prevent the fire from reaching the adjoining buildings. At last, yielding to the almost superhuman efforts of the firemen, the fire was extinguished, leaving only the bare and blackened walls standing as monuments of the destruction that had been wrought. Foremost among the brave fellows who were performing their self-appointed and Herculean duty was a man about thirty-five years of age, stout and muscular in form, and with a good-humored, honest face, that would attract your friendly regard at a glance. He was the most active and energetic man upon the ground, and it could be seen at once, that his whole heart was in the work in which he was then so earnestly engaged.

"That's your man," said the chief, pointing toward him, "and now you can commence upon him as soon as you please."

"All right," answered Everman; "I will see what I can do."

The firemen had by this time, gathered up their hose and were preparing to return to their various houses, and Thomas Nelson, after assisting in this labor until it was completed, left his companions, and proceeded along the sidewalk in the direction of the hotel. Everman walked on slowly behind him, and seeing him enter the building, he followed closely after him. Nelson proceeded to the bar-room and had just tossed off a cooling glass of beer, when the operative made his appearance.

"You seem to be thirsty after your hard work this morning," said the detective, in a laughing tone.

"It was pretty hot work, and no mistake," replied Nelson; "and we were mighty lucky in saving the adjoining houses. I was afraid once they would certainly go."

"Fill up your glass again," said Everman; and Nelson graciously acquiesced. "Yes," continued the operative, "you boys did excellent work, and you deserve great credit for it. I suppose your fire department here is composed entirely of volunteers?"

"Yes, sir," answered Nelson, quite pleased with the encomiums which his pet hobby received; "and a better organized fire department is not to be found anywhere."

"Well," said the detective, as he raised his glass, "here's to the health of your fire laddies; may you never miss a run, and always have as good luck as you did today."

"Good," said the delighted fireman; "I don't know your name, but you're a good fellow, and I am glad to hear you speak so favorably of us."

"My name is Everman," answered the detective frankly. "I only arrived in Woodford yesterday, and expected to meet a friend whose family resides here; but I regret to say I have been disappointed."

"May I ask who you were waiting to meet?"

This was the very question the detective most desired to be asked, and he answered at once.

"Yes. I expected to meet Newton Edwards here, and I have some letters for him from his employer, which he ought to receive."

At the mention of the name, Nelson started in astonishment, and then gave vent to a long, low whistle.

"I am afraid you won't find him here," he said at last.

"Afraid, Mr. Nelson! Why, what's the matter?" quickly inquired the detective.

"Well, sir, I am afraid your friend has turned rascal, and has run away."

"What do you mean?" sharply asked Everman. "Surely, you have no reference to my friend, Newton Edwards?"

"Yes, I mean him exactly. He is a damned thief, that's what he is; and he has broken his wife's heart!"

This was enough for Everman; and in a short time he had learned all that the honest carpenter could tell him. On the evening before, it appeared, Mrs. Edwards had received a letter from her husband, the contents of which had made her frantic with grief, and today she was unable to leave her bed. In this letter he had informed her that he had been connected with the robbery of the bank at Geneva, and that he had succeeded in eluding all pursuit, and was now hiding in some obscure place in the state of New York.

"This is all I know about it," added Nelson, "and I suppose I ought not to tell this; but when a man turns out a damned rogue like that, honest people cannot afford to shield or uphold him in his rascality."

"That's my opinion, exactly," rejoined the detective, "and I am sorry, indeed, for Edwards' wife, although I am free to confess that I have no further sympathy for him."

"I ought not to have told you this," said Nelson, with some compunctions of conscience at his garrulity. "And if my wife was to hear that I had done so, she would take my head off."

"Well, she won't hear of it from me, I can assure you, and I am too much disappointed in my friend to speak of it unnecessarily to anyone."

Their conversation was continued a few minutes longer, and then Nelson, promising to see my operative again, took his leave.

Here was a revelation, which amounted to a direct confirmation of our suspicion regarding Edwards, and was convincing testimony of the fact that he was hiding from the officers of the law. The information about his location, while indefinite, was a surety of the fact that he had not gone west, according to his previous arrangement, and that he must be looked for in the state of New York.

One thing, however, was necessary to be done at once, and that was to keep a sharp lookout for any letter which might be mailed by Mrs. Edwards or any member of her family. There was no doubt that this lady would sooner or later attempt to write to her husband, and that too within a few days. It was therefore of the utmost importance that a close watch should be kept upon all the movements of the members of Mr. Black's household, and then to endeavor to get at the address of any letters which they might attempt to mail.

Everman immediately sent his report of what he had learned to me, and then sought the chief of police in order to enlist his further aid in such efforts as were now necessary to be taken.

When the chief had listened somewhat incredulously to what Everman had been enabled to learn in the few minutes' conversation which he enjoyed with Tom Nelson, he was overwhelmed with surprise at the rapid success he had met with, and he readily proffered all the assistance in his power.

Everman resolved to see Nelson again, and endeavor to induce him to ascertain the exact locality in which Edwards was hiding. The carpenter could not recollect it at the first interview, and was not sure that he had heard it, but Everman concluded to try to jog his memory upon that point still further. He did not have to seek an opportunity for meeting his man, for that evening he received another call from Nelson, who had evidently taken a great fancy to my affable operative. During the conversation that followed, Everman was informed by his new-found friend, that as well as he could recollect the name of the place from which Edwards' letter was posted began with a *"Mac,"* and that was all that could be elicited from him.

Everman gave as his reasons for desiring to learn this fact, that he wanted to write to him himself, and convey the letters which had been entrusted to him.

After spending some time in the vain endeavor to refresh the carpenter's memory, they at length parted for the night.

"Remember, Mr. Everman," said Nelson, as he left the hotel, "if I can find out for you what you want, I will surely do so; but for heaven's sake don't let my wife know it, or I will be scalped alive."

The detective laughingly promised to beware of the sanguinary Mrs. Nelson, and the carpenter went his way.

Chapter VIII

A Plan to Intercept Correspondence — Edwards Fully Identified — A pretty Servant Girl and a Visit to Church.

W hile these events were transpiring at Woodford, William had not been idle in the city. A constant watch had been maintained upon the several premises occupied by the relatives of Newton Edwards, in the hope of detecting some attempt upon their part to communicate with the suspected thief. This at all times is rather a difficult object to achieve, but we have frequently been obliged to resort to this mode of acquiring information from lack of definite knowledge on which to base intelligent action. In order that one of the many of these expedients may be fully understood, a few words in detail may not be out of place. As is well known, the mail of an individual is so sacredly guarded by the laws of the country which govern the postal service, that an attempt to interfere with the letters of another is regarded as a felony and punished with severity. Of course, therefore, no efforts of ours would be directed to the obtaining or opening of any letters which might be mailed to the suspected individual. Our object was simply to obtain the addresses upon the envelopes, if possible, and then to search out the parties to whom they had been consigned. In this instance our manner of proceeding was quite simple, but it required that it should be managed with great care and without exciting the suspicion of anyone. For this purpose each of the operatives, detailed for this duty, was provided with a number of envelopes of a peculiar size and color, and all addressed to fictitious persons. Our plan was, that if anyone of Edward's relatives deposited a letter in any of the street boxes, the operative should be on hand and be prepared to drop his letter into the box immediately on the top of it. Another operative was then to await the visit of the postman on his round for collection, when he would step up to him and making a pretense of a mistake in the address of a letter which he had mailed, would from its position be enabled to obtain a glimpse of the suspected letters below, and their addresses.

This watch was maintained unceasingly for several days without result, and it appeared either that the family were unaware of Edwards' hiding place, or else that they were fearful of being watched, and avoided communicating with him on that account.

In the meantime, William received another visit from Mr. Silby, the president of the despoiled bank, who stated very reluctantly, that he and Mr. Welton, the cashier, during the absence of Eugene Pearson from the bank, had attempted the feat of loosening the screws upon the lock of the vault, and had been unable to do so. They had exerted their strength to the utmost, and the screws had sturdily resisted their efforts. He was therefore compelled to admit that thus far the suspicions against young Pearson appeared to be well founded, and that the screws had evidently been loosened before the prisoners were confined in the vault, in order to allow them to escape, should the atmosphere prove too oppressive for their safety. Mr. Silby also stated, that he had obtained an interview with a Mr. Crampton, the president of the bank at Independence, where it was learned that the parents of Newton Edwards resided, and that without divulging any of our plans regarding that young man, he had acquired considerable information concerning him. It was learned that Edwards had for some time been regarded as a very fast young man, and several episodes were related of him, in which he had figured in no very enviable light.

His parents were elderly people of eminent respectability, and were much distressed at the actions of their son, from whom they had expected so much. He had begun life with bright prospects, had entered into business with his own capital, but had failed after a short career, owing to his extravagant habits and his inattention to business. After this he had traveled for several firms, and while it was believed he received a large salary, there were many who shook their heads at the stories of his dissipation which reached their ears from time to time.

This was information which was of some value, and opened up the way to accomplish an object which William had long desired. He therefore requested Mr. Silby to introduce John Manning to Mr. Crampton, and directed Manning to accompany that gentleman to Independence, and by their joint efforts endeavor to obtain a photograph of Edwards. This was attended to at once, and in a few days, through the assistance of the sheriff at Independence, we were enabled to secure an admirable likeness of the absconding burglar, although the same had been taken nearly two years prior to this. A number of copies of this photograph were at once printed, and they were furnished to the various operatives who were at work upon the case. Hitherto we had been compelled to rely upon the rather unsatisfactory method of identifying him by description only, and in many cases, except where persons are trained to the work of accurately describing individuals whom they meet, there is danger of not being able to identify anyone who has no very prominent distinguishing marks about him.

The first use to which this photograph was put was to exhibit it to Miss Patton, the young lady who had been assaulted in the bank, and she instantly recognized it as the picture of one of the men who had committed the robbery, and the one who had attacked Eugene Pearson, while the other intruder was engaged in the attempt to gag and bind her. This was very important, and no further efforts were now needed to establish the identity of Newton Edwards, or to connect him with the robbery as an active participant.

After several days of unproductive watchfulness at the city residences of Edwards' relatives, it became apparent that something more decisive would have to be attempted. From the reports of the operatives who had been detailed upon this part of the investigation, it seemed evident that the inmates had become suspicious of the fact that their movements were being made the subject of espionage, and it was resolved to adapt another system of operation, and endeavor to have one of my men enter the family, and by some means establish a friendly footing with its members. By this means he would be enabled, while unsuspected, to learn of the movements of the people whom he was watching.

I did not have far to seek for a man who would fully answer the purpose I had in view, and one who would succeed if success were possible. I had tried him in several operations where this kind of work was necessary, and he had invariably accomplished what had been delegated to him to perform. I therefore called Harry Vinton into my office, and stated to him the nature of the mission upon which he was to be sent. He was a handsome, jolly, quick-witted and intelligent young fellow, who had been with me for a long time. Entering my employment as an office boy, and evincing a decided task and talent for the profession of a detective, he had continued in my service, until at this time he was quite an adept in his particular line, and many a successful operation had been largely due to his intelligent efforts, while far removed from the directing eye of myself or my superintending assistants. His manners were frank and easy, and among the ladies he was a general favorite, therefore, I concluded to entrust him with the task of obtaining admission into the residence of the sister of Edwards, on Logan Place.

Our operatives had reported that at this house there was employed, in the capacity of domestic, a young and handsome girl, whose conduct as far as could be judged was exemplary in the highest degree, and informing Vinton of this fact, William inquired if he thought he could manage it successfully.

A merry twinkle shone in Vinton's eyes for a moment and then he answered:

"I think I can, sir; and I am willing to make the attempt."

"Very well," replied William, laughing. "Only look out for yourself. I hear she is a very charming young girl, and you may find yourself in earnest before you are aware of it."

"Perhaps I may," said Vinton, "and perhaps I might not do better than that if I tried."

"All right," said William; "I will not burden you with instructions at present, and you will proceed according to your own judgment, only remember what we want to discover, and succeed if you can."

With these words Vinton took his departure.

A few days passed uneventfully by and no report came from Vinton. He was evidently looking over the ground, and as undue haste would avail nothing in a matter of this kind William forbore to push him.

Vinton, however, had not been idle, and his inquiries had developed the fact that the young servant of Mrs. Andrews was a regular attendant at church on Sunday afternoon, when she was allowed her liberty from her domestic duties.

The following Sunday, therefore, found him wending his way toward the church. The day was bright and balmy, and the streets were thronged with pedestrians all bedecked in their Sunday attire, and apparently enjoying to the full their day of rest.

Vinton reached the church, a magnificent structure, with its many spires glistening in the rays of the sun, and its chime of bells which were ringing out their harmonious cadences upon the air. He had been fortunate to find among his acquaintances a young man who also attended this church, and in his company he repaired to the sacred edifice, and joined in the services of the hour. When the last hymn had been sung and the congregation had been dismissed, Vinton and his companion hurried out to the sidewalk, where they could observe all who came out.

Soon the doors were filled with little groups of men and women, all exchanging friendly greetings, and indulging in pleasant gossip before seeking their homes, and to the intense delight of Vinton, he noticed among a company of young ladies, the face and form of Mary Crilly, the pretty servant of the sister of Newton Edwards.

Finding his gaze riveted upon this group, his companion lightly pulled him by the arm, exclaiming:

"What's the matter, Vinton. Has Mary Crilly captivated your senses?"

"I don't know who you allude to, but there is one of the prettiest girls I have seen for a long time."

"I know who *you* mean, though," said his companion laughingly, "and she is one of the nicest girls I know. Although she is simply a servant, she is both pretty, intelligent and industrious."

"Do you know her?" asked Vinton, both delighted and surprised.

"Certainly I do," answered his companion; "her name is Mary Crilly, and she is living with a family on Logan Place."

"Can't you introduce me?" inquired Vinton anxiously.

"Yes, if you want me to; that's my sister she is talking to now, they are fast friends, and Mary will probably spend the evening at our house. Come along, and perhaps you will lose your heart."

The apples had certainly fallen right into his lap, and fortune had favored him this time, if never before.

Stepping up with his friend, Vinton was soon made acquainted with the pretty young domestic, and in a short time afterward was walking by her side in the direction of his friend's house, where Mary was to spend the afternoon and evening.

Strange as it may appear, young Vinton, when not on duty, associated freely with his companions, not one of whom suspected the business in which he was engaged. They only knew that he was employed in an office "down town," and that frequently he was required to be absent from the city for weeks. In a large city, however, there is not the same inclination to inquire about the private affairs of one's neighbors, and hence he had been able, for prudential reasons, to avoid announcing his real occupation, and was not compelled to make a social hermit of himself because of his profession.

Being pressed to remain at the house of his friend, Vinton cordially accepted the situation, and devoted himself to the fair Miss Crilly so assiduously that he soon was in high favor with that young lady. After an enjoyable afternoon, he had the pleasure of escorting Miss Crilly to her home, and when he left her at her door, he was gratified to receive an invitation to call again, which he joyfully accepted, and resolved to take advantage of at an early date.

Thus far we had been successful; we had obtained a photograph of Edwards, which had been promptly recognized. We had learned from his wife that he was hiding in the state of New York; and we had reliable men carefully posted in such a manner that in a very short time definite information must assuredly be obtained.

Chapter IX

Waiting and Watching — Two Letters — Newton Edwards'
Hiding-Place Discovered.

*H*arry Vinton continued his attentions to the fair young domestic, and in a few days he invited her to accompany him to the theater. Edwards' sister, Mrs. Andrews, was present when this invitation was extended, and having formed a very favorable opinion of my good-looking operative, she at once consented, and Mary blushingly signified her inclination to accept his escort. His deportment toward Mrs. Andrews was most deferential and polite, and in a very short time he had quite won her kindly regard. This, of course, was precisely what he was most desirous of accomplishing, and he improved every opportunity that offered to ingratiate himself into the good opinion of Mary's mistress. So agreeably and gentlemanly did he conduct himself that ere a week had elapsed he was quite graciously received, not only by the pretty young servant girl, but by the members of the family as well. Mrs. Andrews, who appeared to be a kind-hearted lady, although seemingly oppressed with some trouble, which was not made apparent, was deeply interested in Mary's welfare, and had taken especial pains to cultivate Vinton's acquaintance. This was done evidently with the view of satisfying herself as to the sincerity of his intentions toward the girl, and to advise with her in the event of her discovering that he was an unworthy suitor for her hand.

Vinton lost no opportunity to advance his friendly footing in the family, and frequently offered his services to Mrs. Andrews in the way of performing trifling commissions for her, which he could execute while on his way to and from his daily labor.

From Mary, Vinton learned that the family were in much distress regarding a brother of Mrs. Andrews, but what it was she could not tell.

He also learned that this brother (who was none other than Newton Edwards), and his wife had resided with the family for some time, but that Mrs. Andrews was very unfriendly to the young woman, and scarcely treated her with the respect which was due to her brother's wife. The young lady was very unhappy, Mary said, and several times she had seen her weeping bitterly in her room. Thus matters continued until on one Saturday morning, but a short time previous to this, the brother came home intoxicated, and abused his wife in a dreadful manner, and after ordering her to return to her family, had left the house, and had not been seen since.

"What has become of the young lady?" inquired Vinton, after he had expressed his sympathy for her unfortunate condition.

"Oh, her brother came for her that very afternoon, and after expressing his mind pretty freely to Mrs. Andrews, he took her to his home, somewhere away from the city."

"Did her husband go away, too?" asked Vinton.

"Yes, he went about the same time, and has not been here since."

"Do the people in the house know where he is?" inquired Vinton.

"I don't think they do," answered the girl, "and they are very much worried about him. There was a letter came from someone the other day, and ever since that time Mrs. Andrews has been in great trouble. She does not tell me anything about it, but I think it is about her brother."

"That's very strange, isn't it?"

"Yes, and what is more so," answered the girl, "for several days past there have been several men about the neighborhood who are strangers, and Mrs. Andrews is very much frightened about it. She is afraid to go out of the house, and seems almost afraid to move."

"Does she think they have anything to do with her?" asked Vinton, surprisedly.

"Oh, I don't know about that; but it is a very unusual thing to have strange men loitering about our neighborhood, and she feels very nervous about it."

Vinton expressed his profound sympathy for the unfortunate family, and without hinting any suspicion that anything of a criminal nature had occurred, he parted from the young lady and returned to his home.

A few evenings after this, Vinton again called upon Mary Crilly, and while he was conversing with her, Mrs. Andrews came into the room.

"Mr. Vinton," said she, "before you go, I want to give you a couple of letters to post for me, if it is not too much trouble."

"Certainly not," he replied, "anything I can do for you, Mrs. Andrews, will be cheerfully done by me, I assure you."

"Thanks," said the lady, "I will have them ready before you leave, and would like to have them posted this evening."

"I will attend to it, madam," said Vinton respectfully.

After passing a pleasant hour with Mary, Mrs. Andrews returned, and handed Vinton two letters which he placed in his pocket without looking at the addresses, a proceeding which he noticed gave Mrs. Andrews some degree of pleasure. After a few moments' further talk he took his leave, and hastened to the agency. Here he was fortunate enough to find my son William, and he immediately produced the two letters and laid them upon the desk.

"I don't know whether there is anything in these or not," said he, "but I thought I had better let you see them."

William took up the two envelopes, and looked at their addresses. With a start of surprise, he read the superscriptions. One of them was addressed to "William Amos, McDonald, New York," and the other to "Newton Edwards, Denver, Colorado, care Windsor Hotel."

Here was a dilemma! Could it be possible that Newton Edwards, knowing that the detectives were upon his track, would continue to use his own proper name, and have letters addressed to him in that open manner? This was certainly a most foolhardy thing for a sensible man to do, who was seeking to evade the officers of justice. Was it not more reasonable to think that Mrs. Andrews, taking alarm at the possibility of the actions of herself and family being watched, and being fully aware of the crime her brother had committed, would be advised to direct her letter to him under an assumed name?

A glance at the inside of these neat little envelopes would have satisfied all doubts upon the question, but with a delicate regard for the privacy of individual correspondence, William would not have opened them for any consideration.

"This is very clever," said he; "but I am afraid Mrs. Andrews is not quite sharp enough for us this time. However, we will sleep upon the matter, and see what will turn up by tomorrow."

The next morning all doubts were set at rest. Mr. Warner, my son William and myself, were seated in my office discussing this question. We were unanimous in our opinion that the letter addressed to Newton Edwards was a decoy; and with Everman's information before us, that Edwards was hiding somewhere in New York state, which began with a "Mac," all of us were convinced that the second letter alone was deserving of serious attention.

While we were thus debating the question, the mail brought us a report from William Everman at Woodford, that settled all doubts. Mrs. Edwards, he stated, had been seen to mail a letter that evening, and after a serious effort, Everman had obtained a glance at the address. It was as follows:

William Amos,
McDonald,
New York

"That settles it!" said I; "send at once to McDonald, and my word
for it, Edwards will be found."
Whether I prophesied true or not, will soon be seen.

Chapter X

*The Burglar Tracked to His Lair — The Old Stage Driver — A Fishing
Party — A Long Wait — A Sorrowful Surprise — The Arrest of
Newton Edwards.*

Our plans were soon completed for a visit to the place indicated by
the address upon the two letters. In the meantime, however, I had
telegraphed to the police officials at Denver, and learned from them
that no such person as Newton Edwards had been about that place, or
was known there at all. They also promised that if anyone called for a
letter addressed to that name they would arrest him at once and inform
us immediately.

McDonald, I soon learned, was a little village in the central part of
New York, remotely situated, and with no railroad or telegraph facilities
of any kind. An excellent hiding place for a fugitive certainly, particularly, as I suspected, if he had relatives residing there. Far away from the
swift and powerful messengers of steam and electricity, he might safely
repose in quiet seclusion until the excitement had died away and pursuit
was abandoned. Such places as these afford a secure harbor for the
stranded wrecks of humanity, and many a fleeing criminal has passed
years of his life in quiet localities, where he was removed from the toil
and bustle, and the prying eyes of the officers of the law in the more
populous cities and towns.

Two men were selected for this journey, and their preparations were soon made. That evening they were flying over the ground in the direction of the little hamlet, where they were hopeful of finding the man they were seeking.

As an additional precaution, and fearing that Edwards might not remain in McDonald for any length of time, I telegraphed to my son, Robert A. Pinkerton, at New York city, to also repair, as soon as possible, to that place, and if Edwards was there to arrest him at once, and await the arrival of my operatives from Chicago.

Immediately upon the receipt of this message, Robert left New York city by the earliest train, and without event, arrived at the station nearest to the village of McDonald, which he learned was about twelve miles distant. Here he was obliged to take a stagecoach, and after a long, hot and fatiguing journey of several hours, he arrived about nightfall at the sleepy little village, which was his point of destination. By making inquiries of the stage-driver in a careless manner, and without exciting any suspicion, he learned that there was a constable at that place, and on arriving, he immediately sought out this important official. From him Robert learned that there was a strange young man stopping with an old farmer about two miles out of the village, who had been there several days, and who was represented as a nephew to the old gentleman. Upon showing him the photograph of Edwards, he recognized it at once, and signified his readiness to render any service in the matter which might be required of him. After disclosing as much as he deemed advisable to the constable, whose name was Daniel Bascom, Robert gladly accepted his hospitality for the night, and feeling very tired and weary after his hard journey, he retired to rest, and slept the sleep of the just, until he was awakened in the morning by his hospitable entertainer. Springing from his bed, and looking out at his window, he saw that the sun was just peeping over the hills in the east, and throwing its first faint rays over the beautiful landscape that was spread before him, lighting up hill and dale with the roseate but subdued splendor of its morning beams.

After partaking of a hearty breakfast, Robert and the village constable matured their plans of operation. As a well-dressed city young gentleman might occasion some curiosity in the village, and as young Edwards might take alarm at the unexpected appearance of a stranger in that retired locality, it was decided to make some change in Robert's apparel. The constable therefore very kindly offered him a suit of his clothing, which as the two men were nearly of the same size, and the articles slightly worn, answered the purpose admirably, and in a few moments Robert was transformed into a good-looking countryman, who was enjoying a short holiday after the labors of harvesting, which were now over.

In company with Mr. Bascom, the constable, Robert sauntered into the village. It was a beautiful morning; the air was delightfully fresh and cool, and the rays of the sun danced and glistened upon the dew-drops which sparkled upon every tree and flower. The feathered songsters filled the air with their sweet melodies, and nature with all its gladsome beauty was spread before him. Such a feeling of rest and thorough enjoyment came over him, that it was with an effort, he was able to shake off the pleasures of the hour, and bring himself to the disagreeable business in hand. After a short walk they approached the general store of the little village, which was the lounging-place of all the farmers for miles around. When they arrived they found a motley gathering assembled to witness the great event of the day in this town, the departure of the stagecoach, and Robert was speedily introduced as a relative of Mr. Bascom, who had came to McDonald to spend a few days.

The mail coach was an important institution in McDonald, and was regarded as the great medium of communication between that place and the great world outside. Every morning at precisely the same hour the coach departed, and every evening with the same regard for punctuality the old time-worn vehicle rolled up before the platform in front of the store, to the intense delight and admiration of the assembled crowd.

For nearly forty years had this identical old coach performed this journey, and the same old driver had drawn the reins and cracked his whip over the flanks — I was about to say, of the same old horses. This, however, could not have been so, although the sleepy-looking, antiquated animals that were now attached to the lumbering old yellow coach, looked as if they might have done duty for fully that length of time.

Two young men were already seated in the stage, and their luggage was securely stowed away in the boot. The postmaster — the village storekeeper filled that responsible position — was busily engaged in making up the mail, and old Jerry, the fat good-natured old driver, was laughing and joking with the by-standers, as he awaited the hour for departure. As Robert stepped upon the platform he bestowed a hasty, though searching glance at the two men in the coach, and to his relief found that neither of them was the man he wanted, and he quietly stepped back and watched the proceedings that were going on around him.

The postmaster appeared at last, mail-sack in hand, which he consigned to Jerry's care, and that burly individual clambered up to his place as gracefully as his big body and exceedingly short legs would permit. Seating himself upon his box, he gathered up his reins and shouted a good-natured farewell to the crowd. A quick and vigorous application of the whip awakened the dozing horses so suddenly that they started up with a spasmodic jerk which nearly threw the old fellow from his perch. By a desperate effort, however, he maintained his seat, but his broad-brimmed hat went flying from his bald head and rolled to the ground, scattering in its fall his snuff-box, spectacles and a monstrous red bandanna handkerchief. This little episode called forth a peal of laughter from the by-standers, in which the old man heartily joined.

"Stick to 'em, Jerry!" cried one, "too much oats makes them animals frisky," while another hastened to pick up the several articles and restore them to their owner.

Jerry wiped the great drops of perspiration from his bald, shining pate, as he replied:

"Them hosses are a leetle too high fed, I'll admit, but I'll take some of the vinegar out of 'em afore night, or my name ain't Jerry Hobson."

Everything being now in readiness, he again spoke to his steeds, and this time without mishap, the lumbering old vehicle rattled away on its journey. The little crowd gradually dispersed and soon left Robert and the constable alone with the store-keeper.

"I didn't see old Ben Ratcliffe around this morning," said Mr. Bascom to John Todd, the store-keeper.

"No," answered that individual; "he was here last evening, and said if the weather was fine he was going with his nephew over to the lake, fishing."

"That accounts for it, then," said the constable; "I don't think he has ever missed a day for ten years before."

"No, I don't think he has; but that young Mr. Amos, who is stopping here with him, is very fond of fishing, and the old man promised to take him over to Pine Lake this morning, so 'Uncle Ben' missed the mail for once."

After a short conversation with the store-keeper upon general matters, the two men took their leave. It seemed very evident that as yet there was no suspicion on the part of Edwards, as to the discovery of his hiding place, and here in fancied safety, surrounded by nature in all its beauty, with affectionate relatives, the young burglar was enjoying himself as heartily as though no cares were oppressing him, and no thought of detection ever troubled his mind.

The uncle of young Edwards, it was learned, was a general favorite about the country. A good-natured, honest old farmer, who had lived there from boyhood, and was known to all the farmers and their families for miles around. Even in his old age, for he was long past sixty now, he cherished his old love for gunning and fishing, and held his own right manfully among those who were many years his junior.

It was decided, as a matter of precaution, that they should call at the house of Uncle Ben, in order to ascertain whether he and his nephew had really gone fishing, and to that end the constable harnessed up his horses, and in a few minutes they were on their way to the old farmhouse, which stood at the end of a long shady lane leading off from the main road.

Driving up to the gate, the constable alighted and approached the house, while Robert remained seated in the buggy. In a few moments he returned, and stated that Mrs. Ratcliffe, the good farmer's wife, had informed him that her husband and nephew had gone off before daylight to a lake about five miles distant, and they would not return until late in the evening.

It was deemed advisable not to attempt to follow them, as their appearance at the lake might give the young man alarm, and as they were not sure of any particular place to find them, they concluded to quietly await their return. They accordingly drove back to the village, and Robert returned to the constable's house to dinner. In the afternoon the two operatives whom I had sent from Chicago arrived, having been driven over by private conveyance. Without publicly acknowledging them, Robert gave them to understand that he would meet them at the house of the constable, and upon repairing thither they were duly informed of what had taken place, and instructed as to the plans proposed for that evening.

Nothing of any note transpired during the afternoon, and after sundown the party started out upon their errand. Night soon came on, throwing its sable mantle over the earth, the sounds of the busy day were hushed, and all the world seemed wrapped in the tranquil stillness of a summer night. The stars, in countless numbers, were twinkling and sparkling in the blue heavens above, while the new moon, like a silver crescent, shed its soft light upon a scene of rare beauty and quiet loveliness.

Arriving within a short distance of the old farmer's house, the horses and buggy were secreted in a little grove of trees that skirted the main road, and the men stationed themselves in convenient hiding places along the lane, to await the return of the farmer and his nephew. From the appearance of the farmhouse, it was evident that the fishing-party had not yet returned, and they settled themselves down to a patient, silent waiting, which, as the hours wore on, grew painfully tedious and tiresome. At last, long past midnight, and after they had begun to despair of accomplishing the object of their visit, they heard a faint noise, as though footsteps were approaching.

"Hist!" cried Robert, "someone is coming."

They listened intently, and gradually the noises grew louder and more distinct. As they came nearer the constable distinctly recognized the voice of the old farmer, who was evidently relating some humorous story to his companion, who was laughing heartily. The merry tones of this young man's laugh were as clear and ringing as though he had not a care in the world, and had not committed a crime against the laws of the state. No one, to have heard that hearty, melodious burst of merriment, would have supposed for an instant that it came from the lips of a fugitive from justice.

They were now nearly opposite to the crouching figures by the roadside. The old farmer had evidently reached the climax of his story, for both of them broke out again into a fresh burst of violent laughter that awoke the echoes round about them.

The laugh suddenly died away, the merriment ceased abruptly, as a dark form emerged from the roadside, and the muzzle of a revolver was placed close to the cheek of the young man, while Robert called out menacingly:

"Newton Edwards, I want you!"

With an exclamation of pain, the young man dropped his fishing-pole and the bucket of fish he was carrying, while a chill ran through his frame, and he shivered like an aspen in the grasp of the determined detective.

The others had now come forward, and as soon as he could recover from his astonishment, the old farmer cried out:

"What does this mean?"

"It means," said Robert coolly, "that we have arrested your nephew for burglary, and that he must go with us."

The moon just then came peeping from behind a cloud, and fell upon the haggard face and wild eyes of the hapless prisoner, who until then had not uttered a word.

"It is all a mistake, Uncle Ben," faltered he; "but there is no use of making a denial here; if the blow has fallen, I must meet it like a man."

The old man, with tears in his honest old eyes, gazed for a moment at his miserable relative, and then, putting his sturdy old arms around him, he turned to the officers:

"Gentlemen, I suppose it is your duty. I have no fault to find. If the boy has done wrong, he must suffer; but bring him to the house now, and in the morning you can go your way."

His offer was accepted, and directing the constable to return to his own home with his carriage, the others walked slowly up the lane toward the house.

But few words were spoken during the night. The old farmer and his wife retired to their room, and during the few hours that remained, their voices could be heard as they sorrowfully discussed the painful situation.

Securing Edwards' effects, which consisted of a small portmanteau, they learned from the honest old farmer, whose word was as true as gold, that nothing else belonging to the young man was in the house. All attempts to induce the young man to speak were unavailing, and they finally let him alone, and during the long hours he maintained a dogged silence. The detectives patiently awaited the dawning of the morn. At last the eastern sky was tinged with red, and the faint beams of a new day came streaming in through the windows of the old-farm house; and then Edwards, after bidding a tearful adieu to his aged and stricken relatives, and accompanied by the officers, left the house and proceeded on his way to McDonald, to commence his journey to Chicago.

Chapter XI

Newton Edwards brought back to Chicago — Attempt to Induce a Confession — A Visit to his Relatives — The Burglar Broken Down.

*I*t was in the grey dawn of the morning when the party arrived at the house of the constable, Daniel Bascom. Here breakfast was prepared, and after full justice had been done to a bountiful repast, an examination of the effects of Newton Edwards was commenced. Ever since his arrest the young man had maintained a rigid silence, not deigning to notice the detectives in any manner whatever. He partook of his breakfast in a dazed, dreamy fashion, scarcely eating anything, and pushing back his plate as though unable to force himself to partake of food. In his satchel was discovered a roll of bank-bills, which on being counted was found to contain a trifle over three thousand five hundred dollars.

Edwards gazed at this money with a greedy, frightened look, like a wild beast at bay, but did not utter a word, as Robert placed it in a large envelope and secured it about his person.

"Will you be kind enough to inform me," said Robert, when this was completed, "how you come to have so much money about you?"

After a moment's hesitation, Edwards replied, doggedly:

"Yes, sir, I will. It is the proceeds of the sale of some property that I owned in the west."

"Very well," replied Robert, finding it useless, at present, to attempt to induce him to tell the truth. "You will have ample opportunity to satisfy a court and jury upon that point in a very short time."

Nothing farther was said to him until the time arrived for departing, and then the party, with their prisoner, walked into the village in order to take the stage for the railroad station at Birmingham.

Before leaving Mr. Bascom's, however, Robert handsomely remunerated the energetic constable for his valuable assistance, and after thanking him warmly for his active and cordial aid in our behalf, requested his company to the village.

As they approached the store, where the stagecoach was in waiting, they found an unusual crowd awaiting their appearance. The news of the robbery and arrest had by some means become known, and the eager faces of nearly three score of curiosity-seekers greeted them upon their arrival.

Old Jerry himself seemed to be impressed with an idea of additional importance, as though he was about to be called upon to perform a noble service of great responsibility to his country, in assisting to convey such a distinguished company in his old coach. The farmers gathered in little groups about the platform, and conversed in low tones, as they furtively regarded with sentiments almost approaching a respectful awe, the unwonted presence of the detectives and their charge. There was an utter absence of the boisterous hilarity which had been manifested on the preceding morning, and one might have thought that they had assembled for the purpose of officiating at a funeral, so thoroughly subdued and solemn did they all appear.

The journey to the railway station was made in due time, and without accident, and the party were speeding on their way to Chicago. Robert forbore to press the young man any further, and let him severely alone during the entire day. During the night they all retired to their sleeping berths, Edwards being securely handcuffed to one of my men, and occupying the same berth with him.

In the morning, Robert noticed a slight change in the demeanor of Edwards, and thought he detected a disposition to converse. He did not encourage him, however, preferring by all means that the advances should be made by the young man himself. Nor did he have long to wait. They procured their breakfast in the dining car, and after the meal was concluded, Robert, without uttering a word, handed Edwards a cigar, which he very gratefully accepted. After sitting quietly smoking for a few moments, he turned to Robert and asked: "Mr. Pinkerton, how did you discover that I was in McDonald?"

"In the same manner in which we have discovered many other things in connection with this robbery," replied Robert. "I may say, however, that the man we came for was William R. Amos; do you know anything about such a person?"

As Robert spoke he gazed scrutinizingly at the face before him, and Edwards winced perceptibly under his glance.

"I can explain that all right," he at length replied, with considerable embarrassment. "I got into some trouble at home with a young lady, and thought it best to leave town for a short time."

"Edwards," said Robert sternly, "falsehood and impudence will not help you in this case, and I wish to hear no more. I have only to say that we have evidence enough against you to insure a conviction, and your only hope lies in making your sentence as light as possible."

"How so?" he asked.

"By telling all you know about this matter. One of your accomplices, we have got dead to rights, and if you won't tell perhaps he will."

"Who have you got?" inquired Edwards, anxiously.

"That I cannot tell you now; our business is with you for the present. I want you to consider this matter carefully. You are a young man yet, and though you have thrown away golden opportunities in the past, you have yet an opportunity to reform your ways, and by assisting the officers of justice in recovering the money which you and your companions have stolen, and in arresting the rest of your associates, you may receive the clemency of the court, and perhaps benefit yourself materially."

Edwards was silent for a long time after this, and it was evident that he was seriously considering the matter. The words of the detective had made an impression upon him, but with the craftiness of an old offender, he was debating a plan by which he might turn his admissions into account for himself. At length he turned to Robert and asked:

"Will I be able to escape if I tell what I know?"

"I cannot promise that. But you are aware that the giving of information which leads to the capture of your associates and the recovery of the balance of this money, will work to your advantage very decidedly in the mind of the judge."

"Very well," said Edwards, with a dogged sullenness, "your advice is very good, but I have no confession to make."

"Take your own course," said Robert, carelessly. "My advice was for your own good, and as you don't seem willing to accept it, I have nothing more to say."

Although he had not accomplished very much as yet, Robert was still hopeful of inducing Edwards to unburden himself; but he resolved to attempt nothing further with him until they arrived in Chicago, where he could be managed more successfully by those who were more fully conversant with the facts in the case. He well knew that we already possessed testimony amply sufficient to convict Edwards of participating in the robbery, but what we most desired was to obtain information concerning his partners in the deed. However, he decided to allow him ample time for reflection and said no more to him upon the subject until they reached Chicago, when he was at once conducted to the agency.

A consultation was immediately held in order to devise the best means to be pursued to induce Edwards to reveal who his partners really were. William at once resolved upon a plan which he was hopeful would lead to good and immediate results. Calling a carriage, he directed the driver to take him to the residence of Edwards' sister, Mrs. Andrews, on Logan Place. On arriving at the house, he found that lady and her daughter at home, and he was immediately ushered into the parlor by the pretty servant, Mary Crilly. Without unnecessary preliminary, William informed the lady that we had succeeded in arresting Edwards for the robbery of the Geneva Bank, and that he was now in custody. He also stated that from information which he had obtained, he was led to believe that his family were perfectly aware of his actions in this matter, if indeed they had not aided him in accomplishing it.

At this point both mother and daughter burst into tears and sobbingly denied any knowledge of Edwards' crime until after he had committed it, and then they could not act as his accusers. Mrs. Andrews finally urged him to visit Edwards' brother, who resided on Freeman street, and hinted that he could tell something about the matter, although she asserted he took no part in it, and knew nothing about it until it had been completed.

Taking it for granted that they had told him all they knew about the robbery, William next hurried to the place of business of Edwards' brother, whom he was fortunate enough to find in his office, and disengaged. He at once stated who he was, and what he wanted to know. Mr. Edwards was at first disposed to deny all knowledge of the matter, but on William's informing him of his brother's arrest, and hinting that he had made a partial confession, he changed his mind and became quite communicative.

The brother then stated that for years he had been troubled with Newton's bad habits and extravagances, although he had never known him to commit a crime until the robbery of the bank at Geneva. He remembered hearing his brother boast once when he was intoxicated, that he could get plenty of money without work; but as Newton gambled a great deal, he imagined that he had alluded to that means of obtaining his money.

"Well," said William abruptly, "I want to know what you know about this robbery."

"I will tell you all I know," answered Mr. Edwards. "Some three or four weeks before I heard of this robbery, Newton was at my house, and was intoxicated. He boasted in his maudlin way that he had an opportunity to rob a bank, and that the cashier was a party to the affair; but I attributed all this to the wild utterances of a drunken man, and paid no further attention to it. On the Saturday night before the robbery took place, however, he came to my house during my absence, and had a companion with him, for whom he made a bed upon my parlor floor. In the morning they went away, and I have not seen him since. My wife informed me afterward that Newton, who was drunk at the time, had told her that the man with him was the one that was to help him to rob the bank, and that she had then ordered both of them out of the house. I did not at any time know where the bank was located, nor did I ever seriously entertain the idea of his attempting anything of the kind; but when I heard of the robbery of the Geneva bank, I at once suspected my brother, and although humiliated deeply at the thought, I could not take any step that would tend to bring disgrace and ruin upon my own family."

Without entering into the question of family honor, William inquired:

"Do you know the man who was with him at your house, and who was to assist in this robbery?"

"No," answered Mr. Edwards. "I never heard his name, and all that I ever knew of him was that he came from Denver, Colorado."

"Can you describe him?" asked William.

"Yes, I think I can," said Mr. Edwards, and he then gave a description of the man, which agreed perfectly with that of Edwards' companion on the day of the robbery.

Having now obtained all the information that was possible to be gained from this source, William returned to the agency, and entered the room where Edwards was confined. He found the young man sitting with his face buried in his hands and evidently in sore distress.

"Mr. Edwards," said William in his quick, imperious manner, "I have just had an interview with your brother and sister, who have told me all they know about this matter. You will readily see what little hope there is left for you if you persist in keeping from us the information which we desire. Whether you confess or not will make but little difference to us now, as sooner or later your associates will be caught, and your refusal to help us will only make it the harder for you. If you don't confess, Eugene Pearson will."

As William uttered this last sentence Edwards started to his feet, and exclaimed:

"My God, you know more than I thought! I will tell what I know."

At last we had succeeded in breaking him down, and there was a gleam of satisfaction in William's eyes as he requested the presence of Mr. Warner and my son Robert, while the story was being told.

Chapter XII

The Confession of Newton Edwards — The foul Plot fully Explained — Eugene Pearson's Guilt clearly Proven — A Story of Temptation and Crime.

*T*he confession of Newton Edwards revealed a history of undiscovered crime that had been carried on for years. Beginning at first in wild and extravagant conduct, which consumed the liberal salary which he received, and then led to the incurring of debts which became pressing and impossible of payment by legitimate means; then followed a thirst for gambling, in which large returns were promised for small investments, and failing in this, came the temptation to crime and his consequent ruin.

How certain it is, that once the downward step is taken, the rest follows swiftly and inevitably, and ruin and disgrace tread swiftly and surely upon the heels of folly and crime. Newton Edwards began life under the brightest aspects. Of respectable parentage, he had enjoyed the benefits of a liberal education, and his first essay in business had been both fortunate and profitable. Beloved by his family, and admired by a numerous circle of friends, he deliberately gave himself up to a life of excess and dissipation, and the end was soon to be a dark and gloomy prison.

I will, however, leave him to tell his own story, and the moral of it is so plain that he who runs may read. We were all seated around the fallen young man awaiting his recital, and after a few moments of hesitation and embarrassment he began:

"I will tell you all there is to relate, and in order that you may fully understand my present situation, I will commence with the first temptations, which finally led to the commission of this crime."

"Yes," said William, encouragingly, "tell us all."

"The robbery of the Geneva bank was planned more than six months ago," continued Edwards, "but its real origin dates back more than a year. At that time I was traveling for a large house in the city, and was receiving a liberal salary. I had a large trade, and my employers were very generous with me. I cannot tell you how I drifted into habits of dissipation, but it was not very long before I found it a very easy matter to dispose of my salary almost as soon as received, and was forced to borrow money of my friends to enable me to maintain myself at all. From that I was tempted to gamble, and being fortunate at the outset, I soon found, as I imagined, an easy way to make money without serious labor; but I speedily discovered that my first success was doomed to be of short life, and I began to lose more money than I had ever won. It was after one of my losing experiences at the gaming-table, and when I was hard pressed for money to meet my immediate wants, that I visited Geneva, for the purpose of selling goods to some of my customers in that place. At that time I made the acquaintance of a young man by the name of Horace Johnson, who was a practicing dentist of that town. Like myself, he was a wild and reckless fellow, given to dissipation and drink, and who, like myself, had been able to conceal the fact from his family and their friends. Johnson's prevailing vice was an uncontrollable passion for gambling, and he had been addicted to this practice for a long time. I afterward understood that he had acquired this habit while attending a dental college in St. Louis, where he had become quite an expert in the handling of cards, and was well posted in the tricks so frequently resorted to by gamblers to fleece their unsuspecting victims.

When he returned from college and established his business in his native town, he became the leader of a set of fast young men, and his office was the nightly resort of his associates, where they played and gambled frequently, until the morning hours drove them to their homes.

"As I have said, I met Johnson at this time, and on my succeeding visit I was introduced by him to Eugene Pearson, the assistant cashier of the bank. That evening we spent together at Johnson's office in drinking and card-playing. Johnson stated that there was an excellent opportunity to make money offered, if we were disposed to accept it. I asked him what it was, and he stated that there were quite a number of well-to-do merchants in the town who were in the habit of meeting in a room which they had furnished for the purpose, and where they played cards for small amounts and for amusement.

"Johnson stated that we could readily make their acquaintance, and once introduced into their games, it would be an easy matter to induce them to play heavily, and then, from his knowledge of gamblers' tricks, we could win their money in spite of them. We all agreed to this, although Pearson declined to become an active player, because of his position in the bank.

"On the next visit I made to Geneva, I remained over Sunday, and being taken to the club, we managed to win several hundred dollars before morning. This continued for some time, and always with the same success, and as a consequence I became more reckless in my expenditure of money than ever before, because I knew of a sure plan to replenish my pockets, when they were empty. Shortly after this, I received a letter from Johnson requesting me to come to Geneva as soon as possible, as he and Pearson had devised another scheme to raise money and wanted my assistance. Being hard pressed at that time, I responded as soon as I could, and in a few days found myself in Geneva, where I was heartily welcomed by both Johnson and Pearson. After supper we met in Johnson's office as usual, and then the plan was made known to me. At first I was startled by the daring proposition, which was nothing more or less than to rob Pearson's bank by means of forged checks. The checks, which had been already prepared by Pearson, were exhibited to me, and I was surprised at the cleverness of the forgery. It looked easy and safe, and I consented. The person selected as the victim was a rich farmer by the name of Henery Sharpless, whose accounts were only settled about twice a year, and consequently detection was not likely to follow very soon. After carefully comparing the forged checks with an old one that was genuine, I no longer hesitated and signified my readiness to try the experiment.

"On the following day, therefore, I went to Johnson's office, and there put on a hickory shirt, a pair of coarse boots and pantaloons, and in a few minutes I was transformed into a veritable countryman. Johnson colored my face and hands with some preparation which made me appear like a tanned and sunburned farmer, and thus equipped, I started for the bank. I was provided with two checks for three hundred dollars each, one of which was to be presented to the Geneva bank, when, if I experienced no trouble, I was to present the other at the Union National Bank, where also Mr. Sharpless kept an account. I had no difficulty whatever in obtaining the money, and after dividing it among the other two, I left town on the first train. I received two hundred dollars for my share, and the forgeries were not discovered until a long time had elapsed, and when it was almost impossible to obtain any information concerning them. To this day I don't believe that any of the officers of the two banks have the slightest idea as to how the thing was done. Soon after this forgery, Johnson left Geneva and located at St. Louis, where he still resides. Emboldened by the success of this first venture, Eugene Pearson, who was really the master-spirit in these later efforts, boldly proposed to rob the bank in which he was engaged, but this was something too audacious to be considered for a moment. At length, by dint of repeated suggestions, Johnson and myself began to give some consideration to the matter, and upon Pearson's assuring us of the perfect ease with which the robbery might be accomplished, we at last began to discuss various plans by which the bank might be robbed. Several ideas and propositions were discussed, but either through fear or some other consideration, they all fell through.

"At last we decided upon the plan which was finally carried out. Johnson and myself were to come to Geneva disguised as much as possible, and after the business of the day was over, and the other officers had gone home, Pearson was to give us the signal that the coast was clear. We were then to enter the bank, the doors of which would be left open, and after securing the young lady and Pearson, we were to rob the vault and place them within it. In order that they might not suffer from their confinement, Pearson was to start the screws in the lock, so that there would be no difficulty in opening the vault, after giving us time to make good our escape. It was understood that there was about twenty thousand dollars in the vault, in gold, silver and notes, and Pearson was to take his share out in advance and hide it, so that no danger should be incurred in the attempt to divide it afterward. As the time approached for carrying this plan into effect, Johnson began to show signs of weakening, and finally declined to have anything to do with it, although he promised to make no disclosures regarding our movements, and to keep our secret inviolate. After Johnson's backing out we did not know what to do, and were just about abandoning the whole thing, when I came across an old traveling friend of mine in Chicago, who had been on a protracted spree, and who was without money and friends, in a strange city, and who came to me to borrow enough to get him home to Denver. The idea at once occurred to me to induce him to join us and in this I was successful, for he was in a desperate state, and anything that promised to furnish him with money would have been greedily accepted at that time. Even after this, however, I don't believe that either of us would have had the courage to carry out the scheme, if we had not continued our drinking, and I don't believe I was sober a single moment until after we had accomplished our object and the robbery was committed. How it was done, you all know, and it is not necessary for me to detail the particulars of an event which will overcast my whole life."

As he ceased speaking, Edwards buried his face in his hands, and wept aloud.

"Who was this man whom you procured to help you?" inquired William.

Edwards hesitated for some time, as though he was loath to divulge the name of his companion, but finally he said:

"His name is Thomas Duncan, and he was in the clothing business, in Denver, Colorado."

"Now tell us how much money you took from the bank, and how it was divided?" asked Mr. Warner.

"There is something about that that I cannot understand," replied Edwards. "From what Pearson told me, there must have been more than twenty thousand dollars in the vault, twelve thousand of which was in gold. The agreement was that Duncan, Pearson and myself were to have six thousand dollars apiece, and the balance was to be paid to Johnson for his silence. Pearson took his share out on the Saturday before the robbery, and when Duncan and I came to divide the money, we found that we were five thousand dollars short. There is only one solution I have to give for this, and that is that Pearson did not act fair with us, and took five thousand dollars in gold more than he was to have done."

"Where did you and Duncan separate after the robbery?" asked William.

"At Clinton, Iowa," was the reply. "Duncan went on toward Des Moines, while I made my way east, where I remained until you found me."

Upon being questioned further, Edwards stated that when he met Duncan, he had a room in the lower part of the city, with a very respectable lady, who rented furnished apartments, and that when he left the city, having no money, he left his trunk and baggage in his room until he could settle for his rent.

This was all that could be gained from Edwards at this time, and it must be confessed was most important. Pearson's guilt was fully proven, and we had a strong clew as to the identity of the third man in the robbery. It is true that he had more than a month the start of us, but we did not despair of finding him at last. In the meantime, much was to be speedily done. Edwards must be conveyed to Geneva at once, Johnson must be arrested at St. Louis, and we must pay our respects to Eugene Pearson as soon as possible. We must also start immediately upon the track of Thomas Duncan, and endeavor to trace him to his hiding place. Everything was therefore made ready for the departure of Edwards, who was consigned to the care of two trusty operatives until evening, when they would take him to Geneva; and William forwarded a telegraphic message to Mr. Silby, at Geneva, to this effect:

"WATCH THAT PACKAGE."

Chapter XIII

Edwards Taken to Geneva — The Arrest of Eugene Pearson — His Confession — More Money Recovered — Dr. Johnson Arrested.

*A*s may be imagined, our detective labors were now but fairly commenced. We had, it is true, succeeded in capturing one of the active participants in the robbery, and in securing nearly four thousand dollars of the money that had been taken. We had also obtained information which would enable us to arrest two more of the parties who were connected with the affair, and perhaps secure an additional sum of money. The information which Edwards had given, however, was of vast importance to us, and enabled us to pursue our further search with a more intelligent knowledge of the parties interested, and with a more reasonable hope of eventual success.

Our suspicions regarding Eugene Pearson had been fully sustained, and while it was a source of regret to us that we would thus prove beyond question the deep guilt of a trusted and respected employé of the bank, and would be compelled to shatter the false foundations of an honorable name, our duty in the premises was clear. Indeed, I have no hesitation in asserting that of all the parties connected with this burglary I had far less regard or sympathy with this deceitful and base-minded young scamp than for any of the others. If Edwards' story was reliable, Eugene Pearson was the arch conspirator of the entire affair, and no possible excuse could be offered for his dastardly conduct. His position in the bank was a lucrative one, and his standing in society of the highest. His family connections were of the most honorable character, while the affection of his employers for him, would certainly have appealed to his sense of honor, if he possessed any, so strongly that guilt ought to have been impossible. For Eugene Pearson there was no consideration of regard in my mind. He had deliberately, and without the slightest cause, violated the most sacred pledges of affection and duty, and had proven recreant to trusts, the very nature of which should have prevented a thought of wrong-doing. He was not dissipated. He did not drink to excess, and his part in the gambling operations of his friends had always resulted profitably to himself. He was a regular attendant at church, conducted himself in the face of all men as one incapable of wrong, and against whom no taint of suspicion could possibly attach. A veritable "wolf in sheep's clothing" was this dishonest man, and as such I felt that he richly deserved the fate that was so soon to overtake him. The day of his hypocrisy and dishonesty was soon to set, to be followed by a long night of ignominy and disgrace which is the inevitable result of such a course of crime as he had been guilty of. I cannot find words to express the detestation in which I regarded this smooth-faced liar and thief, who had outraged all the finer attributes of manhood, and, like the ungrateful dog, had bitten the hand that fed him.

Before taking Edwards to Geneva, it was necessary to make some investigations with regard to Thomas Duncan, who as yet had completely eluded our search, and whose correct identity had until this time, been entirely unknown to us. William resolved, therefore, to improve the time remaining until evening, in making an investigation of the premises previously occupied by Duncan while he was in the city.

Having obtained the exact location of this house, William and Robert repaired thither at once. They found it, as represented, a quiet, respect-

able house, and located in a neighborhood of unexceptionable reputation. Upon being admitted, they requested to see the lady of the house,
who was a quiet, modest-looking widow lady of about fifty years of age.
William introduced his brother as a Mr. Staunton, lately of Boston, who
was desirous of obtaining a pleasant room in that locality, and who
could furnish undoubted references as to respectability and promptness.
They were shown several unoccupied rooms, and finally entered the one
which had probably been occupied by Edwards' companion in the
robbery, for here were two trunks packed and strapped, and apparently
ready to be taken away.

"This room," said the lady, as the two gentlemen noticed the trunks,
"has been occupied by a gentleman who has left the city. These are his
trunks, and he has ordered them to be sent to him."

William had already approached near enough to notice that the
lettering upon the trunks was "T. J. Duncan, Des Moines, Iowa," and
he was convinced that thus far Edwards' revelations had been correct.

"I once knew a man by that name," remarked William, carelessly. "He
traveled in the west for a clothing firm in Philadelphia."

"Oh!" said the lady, "this gentleman, I think, was in the same
business, and perhaps he may be the one you knew?"

"I would not be at all surprised," replied William. "Where is Mr.
Duncan now, do you know?"

"No," answered the lady, "nothing further than that he has ordered
his baggage sent to Des Moines, Iowa."

Finding that thus far Edwards had spoken truthfully, and that no
further information could be elicited from this source, Robert promised
to call again, and the two men withdrew.

At the next corner they found two operatives, who had been directed
to await their appearance, and William, after describing Duncan's
trunks to them, ordered them to keep a sharp lookout for their removal,
and to endeavor to follow them to their destination.

This done, they returned to the agency and completed their arrangements for taking Edwards to Geneva that evening. Operative Everman,
who had returned from Woodford, was directed to proceed at once to
St. Louis, and effect the arrest of Dr. Johnson, the dentist, on a charge
of forgery, and to convey him to Geneva as soon as possible.

It may be stated in passing, that until the confession of Edwards was
made, I had no knowledge whatever of the forged checks which he
mentioned, and the bank had made no efforts to discover the perpetrators of that fraud, which had now so unexpectedly been brought to light.

We had been very careful to keep the fact of Edwards' arrest a
profound secret, and as yet, the officers of the bank and the peaceful

community at Geneva were in entire ignorance of what had taken place. William had telegraphed to Mr. Silby, stating that he would be in Geneva that night, and requesting him to meet him at the train. About midnight, therefore, when they arrived with their charge, there was no excitement or bustle about the place, and even the wakeful and observant railroad men were unsuspicious of the arrival of one of the robbers. A carriage was procured and the party were rapidly driven to the city hall, where, to the surprise of the officials, Edwards was placed in confinement, charged with being a participant in the robbery of the Geneva bank. Fearing that the information would leak out before morning, and that Eugene Pearson would take fright and endeavor to dispose of his share of the proceeds, it was deemed advisable to go at once to his residence and arrest him.

This was done as speedily and quietly as possible, and before the young man was aware of the danger he was in, he was our prisoner. I will not attempt to depict the grief and anger of the family of this unfortunate young man when the object of our visit was made known; but their resentment of our action was just what might have been expected from people who believed implicitly in the innocence of their child, and regarded any attempt to deprive him of his liberty as an unpardonable outrage.

As respectfully, but as firmly as possible William stated his determination to arrest the young man, and informed them that every opportunity would be afforded him to defend himself, and to remove the stain upon his character when the proper time arrived.

Eugene Pearson, the culprit, was the least disturbed of the party. His coolness was imperturbable. He flatly denied all knowledge of the robbery, and in the strongest terms, assured his weeping and grief-stricken relatives of his innocence.

The arrest, however, was quietly accomplished, and Pearson was soon confined beneath the same roof which sheltered his associate in crime, Newton Edwards.

Early the next morning the town was alive with people and the greatest excitement prevailed. The news of Eugene Pearson's arrest had spread far and wide, and a universal sentiment of indignation pervaded the whole community. Angry men gathered at the corners of the street, and threats of vengeance against the officers of my agency were loudly uttered. A lawless outrage had been committed by us, and the righteous indignation of an injured community refused to be appeased. The hotel where my men were stopping was besieged by the angry citizens, and our actions were denounced in the most belligerent manner. Eugene Pearson, in their opinion, was above suspicion; he was their ideal of a moral young man, his father was respected everywhere, and the base and unwarranted invasion of their home by my officers was an indignity which they were resolved they would not allow to pass unpunished. As the morning advanced the excitement increased, and several of the boldest of the angry citizens approached William, and in no complimentary terms expressed their contempt, not only for him individually, but for the methods which had been used to ferret out and apprehend men who were innocent of any wrong.

Under ordinary circumstances William would have resented these insults, and that too in a manner that would have convinced them that he was fully able to defend himself; but realizing the importance of coolness and discretion at this critical juncture, he preserved his good humor, and securing their attention for a few moments, he requested them not to be too hasty in their actions. If Eugene Pearson was innocent, he stated, no serious harm had been done the young man; and if he was guilty, as he could prove in a short time, they would deeply regret the course they were now threatening to pursue.

In the meantime he had not been idle in his attempts upon the stoical firmness of Eugene Pearson himself, and at length the young burglar was broken completely down; he confessed his guilt, and promised to conduct the officers to the spot where he had hidden his share of the booty. In company therefore with two of the officers, he repaired to the barn in the rear of his father's house, and buried in the ground in the yard, they found a sack of coin amounting to the sum of six thousand dollars.

So far, so good. We had now captured two of the robbers, and had secured nearly one-half of the stolen money of the bank.

It is needless to say that immediately following the confession of Eugene Pearson and the finding of the money he had stolen, the opinions of the previously enraged citizens underwent a decided change. If William had desired any evidence of the overwhelming triumph which he had achieved, the deportment of these disappointed men toward him would have fully satisfied him. No longer regarded as a ruthless invader of the privacy of honest homes, and guilty of outraging the finer feelings of humanity, he was everywhere received with the utmost respect and deference, and many apologies were offered for their inconsiderate conduct of a few hours before. And yet it must be recorded, that with this indisputable evidence of Eugene Pearson's guilty participation in the robbery, there yet remained many, who, unable to refute the damning proofs against him, were filled with a sympathetic sentiment of regard for their fallen idol, and their prevailing feelings were those of sorrow and regret.

The majority of them, however, came up by scores, frankly acknowledged their mistake, and freely apologized for their actions, which under the circumstances, were shown to be so hasty and ill-timed.

In a day or two after this, Dr. Johnson made his appearance, under the escort of William Everman; and the delectable trio were placed in separate cells to prevent any collusion between them prior to their examination.

Johnson's arrest had been very easy of accomplishment. He was entirely unaware of what had transpired with the other two, and having had no active participation in the robbery, had imagined himself perfectly secure and had taken no means of escape.

Everman, on his arrival at St. Louis, had, in accordance with my instructions, obtained the assistance of the chief of police of that city, who very cheerfully and cordially volunteered all the aid in his power. Two men were therefore detailed to accompany Everman in searching for Dr. Johnson, and it was nearly midnight before they succeeded in ascertaining definitely where he lived. Shortly after that hour, however, the detectives ascended the stoop of the doctor's residence and requested to see him. He appeared in a few minutes, and as he stood in the doorway, Everman quickly placed his hand upon his shoulder, and informed him that he was wanted at police headquarters. The doctor turned pale at this announcement, and requested an explanation of such an unusual proceeding; but Everman informed him that all explanations would be made in due time, and at the proper place. Trembling in every joint, the discomfited doctor obeyed, and in a few minutes was conveyed to the office of the chief, where he was closely examined, but refused to divulge anything in connection with the robbery of the Geneva bank, and asserted boldly his entire innocence of the charge. Despite his pleadings for delay he was brought to Geneva upon the next train, and in a short time three of the guilty parties were safely in custody.

Our work had thus far been prompt and successful. We had captured the leaders of this gang, and had recovered nearly half of the stolen money. Much more, however, remained to be accomplished, and we determined that our efforts should not be relinquished until Duncan, the remaining member of this burglarious band, had been secured, and some clew to the remainder of the money had been obtained.

Chapter XIV

Proceedings at Geneva — Speculations as to the Missing Five Thousand Dollars — John Manning Starts in Search of Thomas Duncan.

*T*he days which followed the arrest of the three young bank robbers were eventful ones in the history of Geneva. The three youthful offenders, now downcast and humiliated, were afforded a speedy hearing, and when the facts already adduced by us had been received, they were remanded to jail for trial at the next term of court.

It is needless to say that the good citizens of the little town were shocked beyond expression at the unexpected results of our investigation. Both Pearson and Johnson had grown to manhood in their midst, and until this time no taint of suspicion had ever been urged against them. No thought of wrong-doing had ever attached to them, and no shadow had dimmed the luster of their fair fame. Now all was changed, and the irreproachable reputations of days gone by were shattered. Debased and self-convicted, they stood before the bar of justice, to answer for their crimes. Instead of being the objects of admiration, they were now receiving the well-merited scorn of those who had been their friends and neighbors. Scarcely past their majorities, and just stepping over the threshold of life, the future bright with promises and fruitful of golden experiences, they had recklessly thrown all to the winds, and now stood before their former friends with the brand of the felon upon their brows. No sadder spectacle could have been presented, and certainly none more full of warning to the careless youths who thronged the court-room, than the presence of the aged parents of these young men on the day of the hearing. Their cup of bitterness and sorrow was indeed full, and as they raised their tear-stained eyes to their children, there was not one present whose heart did not throb in sympathy for their misfortunes. More especially was this the case with the mother of Eugene Pearson. He was her idol; and until the very moment of his arrest, she had never known him to be guilty of aught that would bring the blush of shame to his cheek. Now, however, the awful revelation came, and the boy on whom she had lavished all the wealth of her true heart's affection was proven, before all the world, to be the blackest of ingrates, and a designing hypocrite and thief. Mr. Silby, too, was much affected by the discovery of Pearson's guilt. His affection and regard were so sincere and trustful, that, had he been his own son, he could not have been more painfully disappointed at discovering his cupidity.

Another interview had been obtained with Edwards at Geneva, and he gave us some further particulars about the course which he and Duncan had taken after having robbed the bank. Shortly after leaving the city of Geneva, they made their way to the railroad, along the track of which they journeyed for some distance. The day was exceedingly warm, and the valise in which they were carrying the stolen money became very heavy and burdensome. Finding it impossible to proceed any further with such a heavy load, they decided to take out all of the money but a few sacks of silver, amounting altogether to about three hundred dollars. This they did, concealing the money about their persons, and then hiding the valise in a corn field which skirted the railroad track. Being furnished with a description of the locality, William proceeded, in company with the officers of the bank, to the place designated, and after a short search, succeeded in finding the satchel which they had discarded. Upon opening it, they found, as Edwards had said, three small canvas sacks containing about three hundred dollars in silver coin. No trace, however, was discovered of the sack supposed to contain the five thousand dollars whose disappearance was still a mystery. Pearson indignantly denied having taken more than six thousand dollars as his share, and this had been found in the yard of his father's house. Edwards was equally positive that he had not seen this sack, and yet the fact remained that there were five thousand dollars in gold coin which could not, as yet, be accounted for.

Numerous theories were now advanced to account for this mysterious disappearance. One was that some outside party had found the valise, and finding the gold, had left the silver in order to make it appear that the satchel had not been disturbed. This was discarded at once, as the position and condition of the valise when found was such that it could not have been tampered with, or even opened. This was a surprising thing to contemplate, for the ground for miles around had been thoroughly searched by hundreds of people, and it was evident that no one had discovered the hiding place of this valise.

Another theory was that it was improbable that the two robbers would overlook a sack containing that large amount of money. Its very weight would have betrayed its presence, and added nearly nineteen pounds to the burden which they carried, and therefore there were still some grounds for entertaining a belief that Pearson had taken more than his share of the booty. To this belief I was not inclined to give much weight, as I felt convinced that Pearson had made a full confession of what had taken place, and had made honest restitution of the money he had taken. Under all the circumstances, therefore, I was inclined to think that Edwards and his companion had taken the gold, and that the capture of the remaining robber would unravel the seeming mystery.

I was further convinced of this by another incident which transpired in this connection. After the valise had been found and returned to the bank, Edwards was taken into the building. The silver coin which had been recovered was placed within the satchel, and handed to him. After taking it in his hand, he immediately exclaimed:

"Why, that isn't nearly as heavy as it was when we left the bank!"

Mr. Silby then brought out a sack containing five thousand dollars in gold, and placed it in the satchel. Again Edwards lifted it, and this time he at once said:

"That is more like it!"

This experience strengthened me in the belief of Eugene Pearson's innocence, and that Edwards and his companion had either lost the gold in some manner, or had disposed of it in some other way.

Acting upon this theory, the ground in the vicinity of the spot where the valise was found was thoroughly searched by both the bank officials and my operatives. All in vain, however; no trace was obtained of the missing sack of gold, and the matter of its loss was as much a mystery as ever.

After the preliminary hearing had been held, the prisoners were removed to the county town, some miles distant, where they were placed in confinement, awaiting the day of trial, which would not take place for some time to come.

While these events were transpiring, we had by no means been idle. Our primary success in arresting the three men thus far secured, had been most gratifying to the officers of the bank as well as to ourselves. Of course I was anxious to continue the search for the missing robber, but no one possessed a better knowledge than myself of the expense and delay that would be contingent upon such an undertaking. I therefore, as was my duty, fully informed the officers of the bank of the difficulty to be encountered if our investigation was continued. More than thirty days had elapsed since the robbery had been committed, the news of the burglary had been spread far and wide, and the information of the capture of the three robbers would be equally disseminated. This would probably place the fugitive upon his guard, and we could not pretend to fix a limit to the time that would be necessary to effect his capture.

All these facts were fully explained to the bank officials, and with the assurance that we would achieve success if it were possible to do so, the matter was left to their decision.

They were not long, however, in coming to a determination, and without hesitation, I was directed to prosecute the search according to my own judgment, in which, they assured me, they placed the utmost reliance.

Thus supported, we made immediate arrangements for a protracted and unceasing search for the fleeing burglar, and before the hearing had taken place in Geneva, operative John Manning had been dispatched to Clinton, Iowa, at which point it was designed to commence operations.

The two operatives who had been detailed to look after the trunks of Thomas Duncan, in Chicago, had also reported the result of their espionage. After waiting for more than two hours, they noticed that an express wagon was driven up before the door, after which the trunks were brought out, placed in the wagon, and rapidly driven away. The operatives followed as rapidly as they were able to do, and ascertained that they were taken to the railroad station for shipment to Des Moines.

As has already been detailed, Edwards and Duncan parted company at Clinton, Iowa, Duncan proceeding west, while Edwards had come direct to Chicago, from which point he had made his way eastward to the little village in New York, where he remained in fancied security until he was so unexpectedly taken into custody.

Clinton, Iowa, was therefore the place from which to trace the flight of the bank robber, and John Manning was dispatched to that place, with full authority to exercise his own judgment about his future course of action.

Chapter XV

On the Track of the Fleeing Burglar — Duncan's Home — Some Reflections.

Within a few hours after receiving his orders, John Manning, satchel in hand, stepped from the train at Clinton, and proceeded to a hotel. It was nearly nightfall when he arrived, and after hastily partaking of his evening meal, he started out to make some inquiries about the man he was in search of. Having by some means gained a knowledge of Thomas Duncan's associates in Clinton, he had no difficulty in finding them, and dropping into a saloon which they frequented, he quietly introduced his name in a casual conversation with the proprietor.

"Do you know Tod?" asked that gentleman, with some surprise.

"Oh yes, very well," replied Manning. "I spent several days with him in Chicago, about a month ago, and had quite a pleasant time."

"Oh, I remember; he stopped here after that, on his way to his home in Des Moines. You must have had quite a time, for Tod looked very much broken up."

"Well, he was on quite a spree, I believe — and so he went to Des Moines, did he?"

"Yes, he started for that point; but I believe he intended stopping some time in Ames, where he has a good many friends."

"Did he say what he intended doing there, or whether he was going on out to Denver?" asked Manning.

"No, I think he said he was going with a fishing-party from there and would be gone several weeks." After stating that he was about to travel in that direction himself, and learning the names of several of Duncan's friends in Ames, Manning left the saloon, and returned to his hotel. Ascertaining that he could leave on a train that night, he hastened to the depot and was soon speeding on his way.

He arrived at Ames in due season, and here he was fortunate enough to find a friend of Duncan's, who informed him that instead of remaining in that city he had only lingered there one day, when he left on a freight train for Des Moines, stating that he was to meet a friend in the latter city and could not wait for the regular passenger train.

Manning without delay then started for Des Moines, and upon arriving there, telegraphed the result of his investigation thus far. In reply he was informed that Duncan's baggage had been sent to Des Moines, and directed to inquire at the office of the American express whether it had been received or delivered.

Immediately on the receipt of these instructions Manning repaired to the express office, and there to his intense delight, he discovered Duncan's trunks among the unclaimed baggage. Making himself known to the express superintendent, who was friendly to our interests, he remained around the office until late in the evening, when as the office was about to be closed, and feeling confident that the trunks would not be called for that night, he repaired to his hotel and sought his much-needed repose.

The following morning he was up betimes, and deferring his visit to Duncan's friends until he had seen the trunks removed, he made his way again to the express office and took up his position as a watcher.

Shortly before noon, a wagon was driven up before the door, and a man presented himself and demanded the trunks in which the detective was so much interested. The wagon bore the name of a grocer, John Miller, and was evidently used in delivering the wares dispensed by the merchant whose name was painted upon its sides. After the trunks had been transferred to the wagon, the driver mounted to the seat and slowly drove away. Manning followed on behind them, and after a short journey, the driver drew up before a handsome residence, surrounded by a beautiful lawn, adorned with numerous beds of bright blooming flowers. The building was a two-story one, with a wide porch extending around three sides, and was evidently the abode of a gentleman in fortunate circumstances. The trunks were removed from the wagon, and carried into the hall, after which the driver returned and drove away. After waiting for some time in view of the house, he saw the trunks taken in, and placed in a front room in the second story.

Having now traced Thomas Duncan's trunks to their destination, and feeling the need of additional assistance, Manning repaired to the office of the chief of police and requested an interview with that functionary. Upon being conducted into the private office of the chief, Manning at once introduced himself, and stated the cause of his appearance in the city. He met with a most cordial reception, and the chief, without hesitation, promised him all the assistance in his power. He had heard of the robbery at the time of its occurrence, and had also read of the capture of the three men, who were suspected of being implicated in that affair. Upon being informed that Thomas Duncan was connected with the burglary, the chief evinced considerable surprise, for he was well acquainted with the young man, and had been for several years, in fact, almost since his boyhood. From the chief, Manning learned that Duncan's parents had lived in the city for a long time, and that "Tod" was rather a wild, careless fellow, who was frequently found in bad company. For a long time the young man and his father had been estranged, owing to the son's persistent course of folly and dissipation. Long and patiently had the old gentleman borne with his son, and had repeatedly opened his purse to liquidate debts which Tod had contracted; but finally, finding it useless to attempt to induce him to change his mode of life, he had forbidden him the house, and had not received him since.

It was barely possible that Duncan might be found in the city, but the chief was inclined to a different belief. In any event, however, it would be useless to seek for him beneath his father's roof. Manning described the house at which the trunks were left, and was informed that it was occupied by a man named John Miller, a grocer, and an intimate friend of Duncan's. Duncan always made Mr. Miller's house his home during his visits to Des Moines, and if anyone was acquainted with his movements, this John Miller ought to be the man.

Instead, however, of calling upon Mr. Miller at once, Manning proposed to shadow the house during the day, in order to see if anyone answering Duncan's description should enter or leave the place. This was deemed particularly advisable, as if Mr. Miller was approached at once, his suspicions might be excited, and if Duncan was in the city the alarm could be given, and he could readily make his escape before we could reach him.

No one at all resembling Thomas Duncan, however, made his appearance during that day, and in the evening Manning repaired to the chief's office, as that gentleman had promised to accompany him on his visit to the friendly grocer.

John Miller and Mr. Wallace, the chief of police, were warm friends, and he felt confident that Miller would not tell him an untruth; but it was deemed best to introduce Manning as a friend of Duncan's, from Chicago, who wanted to see him upon a matter of business. Of course, it had not yet reached the public ear that Thomas Duncan was suspected of complicity in the robbery, as we had kept that fact entirely secret, fearing that a divulgence of Edwards' confession would seriously interfere with our search for the missing burglar, and perhaps prevent us from ever apprehending him.

The two men therefore repaired to the store of the grocer, and were fortunate enough to find him at home. He greeted the chief warmly, and acknowledged the introduction of Manning with good-natured heartiness and sincerity. Inviting them into his private office, Mr. Miller requested to know the nature of their call, and Mr. Wallace at once explained to him what had already been agreed upon. Manning further explained that when he left Duncan, that gentleman informed him that he intended coming to Des Moines, and would probably stop with Mr. Miller.

"Has he been here recently?" asked Mr. Wallace.

"Well, I'll tell you," replied Mr. Miller. "More than three weeks ago he was here. It was about midnight, and I had retired to bed. Suddenly I was awakened by a loud ringing at my door-bell. Hastily dressing myself, I went down, and there, to my surprise, stood Tod Duncan. He was so disguised, however, that I did not recognize him until he addressed me and told me who he was. He was attired in a suit of coarse brown ducking, heavy boots, and a slouch hat; around his neck he wore a large red handkerchief, and he looked more like a German tramp than like my old friend. I felt at once that something was wrong, or that he was in some trouble; so I asked him in, and we went to my room. My family were away at the time, and there was no one in the house but myself, and as he looked tired and hungry, I produced what eatables I had in the house, and he made a hearty meal. After he had finished, he turned to me, and laughingly said:

"'The devil himself wouldn't know me in this rig, would he?'

"I told him I thought not, and then asked him what was the cause of his strange disguise and his unexpected appearance in Des Moines. He told me that he had got into some trouble about a game of poker in Leadville, and that he had shot and perhaps killed a notorious gambler in that city. He wished me to help him, as he was hiding from the officers who were after him, until the affair blew over. He seemed particularly anxious that I should help him to get away. Upon asking him how the affair happened he related the following incident to me. It happened that he was playing a game of poker in Leadville, with a notorious and unscrupulous gambler, and that at one time when there was a large amount of money on the table, this gambler deliberately displayed four aces, when Duncan held an ace which had been dealt to him in the first hand. Upon accusing the gambler of attempting to cheat him, that worthy drew a pistol and attempted to intimidate him. He was too quick for his opponent, however, and quick as a flash, he had fired upon him, and the man fell. Hastily gathering up the money that was upon the table, Duncan succeeded in making good his escape from the house, amid a scene of confusion and uproar impossible to describe. He showed me," continued Mr. Miller, "a considerable sum of money, in proof of his assertion, and of course I have no reason to doubt his word. He further informed me that his trunks were in Chicago and that he was desirous of obtaining them. I provided him with pen and paper, and he wrote a letter which purported to be written in St. Louis and addressed to myself, stating that he was in that city, without a dollar, and requesting me to send for his trunks at Chicago, promising to repay me at an early day. I did not understand this proceeding, particularly as after writing this letter, he gave me twenty dollars, to pay for having his trunks sent to Des Moines, and requested me to allow them to remain in my house until he should send for them. That this letter was intended to mislead someone, I have no doubt; but I was at a loss to understand how it could succeed in its purpose if I retained possession of it. At his request then I enclosed his letter to me to the landlady at Chicago, and I know nothing further about it except that Duncan's trunks arrived today and are now in my house, awaiting his disposition."

"How long did Duncan remain in town at that time?" asked Manning.

"I think he left the next day," replied Mr. Miller. "He left my house on the following morning at any rate, and I learned afterward that he went away with an old friend of his, who is a brakeman on one of the roads here, on the same day that he left my house."

"Do you know who the man was that he went away with?" now asked Mr. Wallace.

"Yes; his name is Bob King, and if I am not mistaken, King obtained a leave of absence from the railroad company for a few days in order to go with Duncan. They hired a horse and carriage and started off in the direction of Grand Junction. King was absent several days, and then returned with the team, stating that Duncan had gone west. I thought this very strange, as, if he had ran away from Leadville, it would certainly be very unwise for him to return. However, I heard no more about him, but I have seen Bob King frequently. He comes in several times a week, and you can most likely find him about some of the boarding-houses around the Union Depot."

This was all that could be gained from Mr. Miller, and after receiving that gentleman's promise to inform Mr. Wallace, in case he should hear anything of Duncan, the two men took their leave of the accommodating and loquacious grocer.

Leaving the chief at his office, Manning resolved to pay a visit to the residence of Duncan's parents. Not, however, to make himself known or to institute any inquiries; but to quietly watch from the outside whatever was transpiring within. He found the house to be a large frame dwelling, with extensive grounds surrounding it; everything evinced the utmost refinement and good taste, and it was evidently the abode of respectability and wealth. The lights were gleaming through the windows of a room upon the lower floor, and Manning quietly opened the gate, and screened himself behind some tall bushes that were growing upon the lawn. Here he was effectually hidden, both from the inmates of the house, and the passers-by upon the street. The scene that greeted his vision was so peaceful and homelike, that Manning was convinced that Duncan's family were entirely ignorant of his movements or his crime. The father, a hale old gentleman with a smiling face, was reading aloud to the assembled members of his family, his wife and two daughters, who were busily engaged in some species of fancy work, so popular with ladies at the present time, and their evident enjoyment of the narrative was unmixed with any thought of wrong-doing or danger to one of their family.

"How strange are the workings of circumstances," thought the detective. "Here is a happy home, a family surrounded by wealth, refinement and luxury, peaceful and contented, while a beloved member of it is now an outcast from the world, a fugitive from justice, hiding from the officers of the law, and vainly seeking to elude the grasp that sooner or later will be laid upon his shoulder."

Silently maintaining his watch until the family retired, the detective slowly made his way to his hotel, and as he tossed upon his pillow, his dreams were peopled alternately with happy home-scenes of domestic comfort and content, and a weary, travel-stained criminal, hungry and foot-sore, who was lurking in the darkness, endeavoring to escape from the consequences of his crime.

Chapter XVI

*Bob King Meets with a Surprise — His Story of Duncan's Flight —
The Detective Starts Westward.*

The most important object now to be accomplished was to secure
an interview with Bob King, the brakeman, who had accompanied
Duncan when he left Des Moines. Manning was convinced that King
was fully aware by this time of the crime which Duncan had committed,
and perhaps for a share of the proceeds, had assisted him in his flight
from justice.

Early on the following morning, therefore, he left the hotel, and
started off in the direction of the depot, resolved to make a tour of the
numerous boarding-houses before calling upon the chief of police. He
had already obtained an accurate description of the man he was in search
of, and had no doubt of recognizing him, should he be fortunate
enough to meet him. Passing quietly along, he came to the large
switch-yards, and here he was almost deafened by the rumble and noise
of the trains, and the screeching and puffing of the engines. Here
Manning paused awhile in the hope of seeing his man among the
number of brakemen engaged about the yard; but finding no one that
answered his description, he approached a party of men standing near,
and inquired:

"Can you tell me where I will find Bob King?"

"Bob is not working today, and you will probably find him at the
Union House, yonder," was the reply, as the man stretched his dirty
finger in the direction indicated. Thanking the man, he passed through
the yard to the street upon the opposite side. Here he found a long row
of houses of various descriptions, but all of them apparently occupied
as eating-saloons, boarding-houses and hotels. On the corner of the
street, and directly opposite from where the detective stood, was a low,
dingy-looking frame building, with the name of Union House painted
across the front.

"Here we are," said Manning to himself, "and we will soon ascertain if Mr. King is about."

So saying he crossed the street and entered the office or waiting-room of the hostelry. An old settee, a half-dozen or more well-whittled wooden armchairs, a rusty stove set in a square box filled with saw-dust, were about all the movable furniture which the room contained. In the corner, however, was a short counter behind which, arranged on long rows of hooks, were suspended a number of hats, caps and coats of a decidedly miscellaneous character.

An ancient-looking register, filled with blots and hieroglyphics, lay upon the counter, and as the room was empty, Manning walked toward the open volume and examined the names inscribed thereon. Under the date of the preceding evening, he found the name he was looking for, and a cabalistic sign on the margin designated that he had lodged there the night before and indicated that he might still be in the house.

While he was thus standing, a frowsy-headed young man, whose face was still shining from the severe friction of a coarse roller-towel, which hung behind the door, entered the room, and saluting the detective familiarly, proceeded to comb his hair before a cracked mirror that hung behind the desk. After he had hastily finished this operation, he turned again to Manning, who had been smilingly observing his movements.

"Have you had breakfast, sir? last table just ready."

"Thank you," replied Manning, "I have already had my breakfast. I am looking for a man who is stopping here, by the name of King."

"What's his first name — Bob?"

"Yes, that's his name. He is a brakeman on the road."

"Oh, yes, Bob's here. He's eating his breakfast now. Just sit down, he'll be here directly."

After waiting a few minutes, a tall, broad-shouldered young man, of rather good-natured and intelligent appearance, entered the room, and taking a cap from one of the hooks upon the wall, placed it upon his head.

It did not require the rather officious indication of the young clerk to induce the detective to recognize the newcomer as the man whom he was most desirous of seeing; his appearance tallied precisely with the description of him which he had previously obtained.

Stepping quietly up to the young man, the detective said, carelessly:

"Your name is Bob King, I believe?"

Somewhat confused by the abrupt salutation, the young fellow replied, rather awkwardly:

"Yes, that's my name; but you've got the brakes on me, for I don't remember that I ever saw you before."

"Perhaps not," answered Manning, "but I want to have a little private conversation with you for a few minutes. Can we go somewhere where we will not be interrupted?"

"Why, yes," responded the other, still evidently ill at ease, "come in here." And turning about, he led the way through a door across the hall, and entered a small and plainly furnished sitting room.

"Wait," said Manning, as if suddenly conceiving an idea. "The morning is pleasant, and I have a good cigar here; suppose we take a short walk together. We can talk as we stroll along."

"All right," said King, as he took the proffered cigar, and lighting it, they went out of the hotel into the street.

Mr. Robert King eyed the detective furtively ever and anon, and seemed to be impatient for him to begin the conversation, and inform him what it was all about. There was, however, such a perfect air of ease and unconcern about Manning, that the young brakeman felt impelled to accompany him whether he would or not. Manning led the way in the direction of the office of the chief of police, and after they had fairly started, he turned to his companion, and good-naturedly said:

"Mr. King, I suppose you are quite anxious to know who I am, and what is the nature of my business with you?"

"Well, yes," answered King, smilingly, for the *sang froid* of Manning had quite won his heart. "I would like to know both of those things."

"Well," said the detective, "my name is John Manning, and I am a native of Chicago. I am an intimate friend of 'Tod' Duncan's, and want to know where to find him."

"You will have to ask somebody that can tell you, then," answered King, who had now fully recovered his composure, "for I don't know anything about him."

"Why," ejaculated Manning, as though quite surprised at the information, "I thought that you and Tod went off on a hunting or fishing party a few weeks ago, and that you came home, leaving Tod to continue his journey alone."

"That's a mistake," said King, "and whoever informed you to that effect was as much mistaken as you are."

Mr. King was evidently trying the good-natured game of bluff, and Manning noticed with some satisfaction that they were now approaching very near to the office of Mr. Wallace.

"See here," said he, suddenly turning on his companion. "Mr. King, this won't do. Duncan is wanted for the Geneva bank robbery. He was here three weeks ago, and you were with him. You got him out of town, and if you are not disposed to be communicative, I have simply got to place you under arrest."

The change in King's manner was very complete. He was utterly surprised and nonplused, and before he could answer a word Manning placed his hand on his shoulder and said, peremptorily: "Come in here, Mr. King; perhaps Mr. Wallace can loosen your tongue."

They were now directly in front of the office of the chief, and King knew that any attempt at resistance would be futile, and decidedly unwise, so he deemed it best to submit at once.

"Don't be too hard on a fellow," said he at last. "I have a good position and I can't afford to lose it. If you will give me a chance, I will tell you all I know."

"Very well, come right in here," said Manning, "and if you tell me the truth, I promise you no harm will come to you."

In a few minutes they were closeted with the chief, who knew King very well, and who added his assurances to those of Manning, that if he would unburden himself fully, no danger need be apprehended.

"I want to say first," said King, at last convinced that it would be better to make a clean breast of the whole matter, "that what I did, was done in good faith, and I only thought I was helping a friend who had got into trouble through acting in self-defense."

"Very well," said Manning, "we will admit all that, but tell us what you know."

"Well," answered King, after a pause in which to collect himself, "It was about three weeks ago, that Duncan came to the city, and knowing where I stopped, he came to see me. I happened to be in from my run when he called, and he wanted to know if I could get a leave of absence for a week, as he wanted to go on a fishing trip and would pay all the expenses. I went to the master of transportation and found no difficulty in obtaining my leave, and then I saw Tod and told him I was at his service. We then procured a team, guns, fishing-tackle and provisions, not forgetting a good supply of smoking and drinking articles, and the next day started off in the direction of Grand Junction. Before we started, Duncan told me about getting into a scrape over a game of cards at Leadville, and that he had shot two gamblers and was keeping out of the way until the excitement over the affair had died out."

"Duncan has raised one man, I see," laughed Manning. "When I heard this story first, he had only killed one gambler in his fight over the cards."

"Well, I am telling you what Duncan told me," answered King.

"That's all right," said Manning quietly, "but suppose you go ahead and tell us what he told you about robbing the Geneva bank."

The cool assurance of the detective, and the easy assumption with which he stated his conclusions, so disconcerted King, that he was speechless for a few moments. Recovering himself quickly, however, he answered doggedly:

"Well, I intended to tell you the whole story, and I was simply telling it in my own way."

"Go on, Mr. King," said Manning, "all I want is the truth, but the card story won't do."

"I guess it won't do me any good to tell you anything else but the truth," rejoined King. "Well, Tod told me about this shooting business before we started, and of course I believed it. I noticed, though, before we were away from the city very long, that there was something else on his mind, that made him very uneasy, and gave him a great deal of trouble. He was moody and silent for hours, and it was only when he drank a great deal that he was at all lively, or seemed like his old natural self. Finally, on the morning of the third day, I put the question fairly to him, and he then told me what he had done. He said he and two others had robbed a bank, and that he was making his way westward. He was resolved not to be captured, and said that no two men should take him alive. He then told me that he wanted me to take the team back to Des Moines, and that he would take the train at Grand Junction, and try to make his way to Manitoba. We parted company at the Junction, where Tod took the train for Sioux City. He paid all the expenses of the trip and offered to give me some of the money, but I refused to accept any, and told him what I had done was done simply for friendship."

"How much money did Duncan have at that time?" asked Manning.

"He had nearly four thousand dollars, I should judge," answered King.

"Did he say who assisted him in this robbery?"

"Yes; he told me that a man by the name of Edwards was one, and that the assistant cashier of the bank was the prime mover in the whole affair. He also said that the cashier had not played fair, but had taken out twelve thousand dollars in gold instead of six thousand. He was very bitter against this man, and said he believed that he would give them all away to save his own neck, if it came to the pinch."

After some further conversation, which convinced Manning that King was telling the truth and that he was entirely ignorant of Duncan's hiding place, the young brakeman was allowed to go his way, with the understanding that they were to meet again in the evening.

Manning now hastened to the telegraph office, and a cipher message, containing in brief all he had thus far learned, was soon upon its way to me.

My reply was to the effect that he should again see King, and inquire if Duncan had mentioned anything about the valise which they had carried away from Geneva. Then to endeavor to obtain a photograph of Duncan, and finally thereafter to lose no time in starting out for Sioux City.

I was considerably exercised about this missing package of gold. I could not believe that Pearson had taken it, although both Edwards and Duncan appeared to be positive of it. The young cashier now seemed to be too utterly crushed down and humiliated to permit me to believe that he had lied still further, and that he was still keeping back a portion of the plunder he had secured. Still, however much I was desirous of discarding such a belief, I was resolved to leave no stone unturned in order to explain the mystery. I felt positive that some explanation would yet be made that would account for this package, and in a manner that would not connect Eugene Pearson with its disappearance. Up to this time, however, we were as far from the truth in this connection as when we commenced, and I could do no more than await the arrest of Duncan, before the matter could be definitely settled. I came to this conclusion on the assumption that all the parties thus far had told the truth, and it seemed to me that one or the other of them must certainly be mistaken in their original impressions.

This theory, however, yet remained. Edwards and Duncan might have obtained the money, and being still under the influence of the liquor they had drank, and excited over what had transpired, had thrown away the valise, and at that time it might still have contained the gold.

In accordance with my instructions, Manning remained in Des Moines two days succeeding this, but was unable to learn from King that Duncan had mentioned the valise in any manner whatever.

In his attempt to obtain a photograph of Duncan, however, he was more successful, and with the assistance of Capt. Wallace, he was fortunate enough to be placed in possession of a very excellent picture of young Duncan, which had but recently been taken. This accession to his stock of knowledge was destined to play an important part in his continued search after the fugitive burglar. Finding that nothing more could be learned in Des Moines, and receiving assurances from the friendly chief that any information would be forwarded to him at once, Manning departed from the home of the youthful law-breaker and started for Sioux City.

Chapter XVII

Manning Strikes the Trail — An Accommodating Tailor — Temporary Disappointment and final Success — The Detective reaches Minneapolis.

*A*ugust, with its hot, sweltering days, when the very skies seemed to be a canopy of lurid, quivering heat; and when every breeze seemed freighted with a depressing warmth that almost rendered labor impossible, had passed away, and we were now in the enjoyment of the clear, cool days of September. The skies were bluer, the air was purer, and the beautiful, golden autumn was welcomed with a grateful sense of pleasure and relief. Nearly a month had now elapsed since the robbery of the Geneva Bank, and, although we had accomplished much, our work was not yet completed. Thomas Duncan was still at liberty, and our task was yet unfinished. I have already, as briefly as I could, related the various events which had transpired since the robbery, and detailed the efforts which we had thus far made toward accomplishing the capture of the perpetrators of this crime. Of Thomas Duncan, however, I had learned comparatively little, and of his movements still less; and yet, at times, I found myself indulging in feelings of sympathy for the young man, who had so recklessly and inconsiderately thrown away the best chances of his life. Of a careless disposition and inclined to folly, I was convinced that until this time he had never stooped to commit a crime. This was his first flagrant violation of the law, and when I thought of him a hunted fugitive, seeking to hide himself from the vigilant eyes of the officers of the law, and of the quiet, peaceful and happy home of his parents, I could not repress a feeling of regret and sorrow for the wayward youth in this, the hour of his humiliation and trial. Far different from Eugene Pearson, who had no cares and no temptations to commit crimes, and who had practiced a scheme of vile deception and ingratitude for years, Thomas Duncan had been found in a moment of weakness and desperation, and under the influence of wily tempters, had yielded himself up to their blandishments, and had done that which had made him a felon. As to Eugene Pearson, the trusted, honored and respected official of the bank, who had deliberately planned and assisted in this robbery of his best friends, I had no words of palliation for his offenses; but for "Tod" Duncan, the weak and tempted victim of designing men and adverse circumstances, I experienced a sense of sympathy which I could not easily shake off.

Where was he now? Perhaps hiding in the forests of the far west, amid the barbaric scenes of savage life; perhaps giving himself up to a reckless life of dissipation, seeking in the delirium of intoxication a forgetfulness of the deed he had committed, and of the consequences which must befall him. How many long, weary nights since he fled from Geneva, with his ill-gotten booty, had he, even in the midst of a bacchanalian revel, started suddenly, as if in fear of the officer he so much dreaded, and then with a boastful laugh drank deeper to drown the agonies that oppressed him? Perhaps, on the other hand, the first step taken, the rest had come easy and without effort, and he had already become hardened and reckless. Whatever might be the case, we were as yet uninformed, and operative John Manning arrived in Sioux City with no definite clew to the missing man.

Seeking, as before, the assistance of the police authorities, Manning proposed to make a tour of the so-called houses of pleasure, which infest all cities, deeming it most likely that he would obtain some traces of Duncan by that means. This proved successful in a comparative degree, for in one of these places Manning found a gay young cyprian, who recognized Duncan's picture immediately. A bottle of very inferior wine at an exorbitant price was ordered, and under its influence the girl informed the detective that Duncan had come there alone one evening about two weeks prior to this time, and that she had accompanied him upon a drive. They had become quite familiar during their short acquaintance, and Duncan drank a great deal. On the following morning he had left the house, and stated that he was going to leave the city that day. Further than this, the girl could not say, and Manning must needs be content with even that trifling amount of encouragement for the present.

Manning had also been provided with a facsimile of Duncan's handwriting and signature, and he carefully examined the registers of the several hotels, in order to discover whether he had stopped at any of them under his own or any fictitious name which resembled in any manner the one he bore, but without any success whatever.

On returning to the hotel, he occupied himself debating as to the best movement to make next. He was surprised on arriving there to find a telegram from Capt. Wallace awaiting him. On removing the enclosure he found a message informing him that Duncan had an acquaintance in Sioux City whose name was Griswold, and who was engaged in the tailoring business at that place.

Aided by this important piece of intelligence, the detective was not long in finding the establishment presided over by Mr. Griswold. That gentleman was located in the business section of the city, and his neatly arranged store was well stocked with goods of excellent quality and apparently of recent style. On entering the shop, Mr. Griswold was found perched on a table in the rear, his legs crossed, and with nimble fingers was engaged in the manufacture of some of the articles of his trade. He was a small, sharp-featured man, about forty, with a shrewd though not unpleasant face, and as he came briskly forward to greet a prospective customer, his countenance was wreathed in a smile that was almost irresistible.

"Can I do anything for you this morning?" was the polite salutation of the little tailor.

"Yes," replied the detective. "I want to look at some goods that will make a good suit of clothes."

"Certainly," replied the knight of the shears. "I have some excellent styles here, and I am sure I can give you your full satisfaction."

"I have no doubt of that," said Manning pleasantly. "I have been recommended here by my friend Tod Duncan, and he speaks very highly of you."

The face of the little tailor was again wreathed in smiles, as he delightedly inquired:

"Do you mean Duncan, the traveling man from Des Moines?"

"Yes," replied Manning, "that's the man; I am a traveling man myself, but in a different line, and I expected to meet him in this city, but I was disappointed. I guess he must have got ahead of me."

"Let me see," said Mr. Griswold, with his needle-pricked finger pressed against his nose. "He was here about two weeks ago, I guess."

"Do you know which way he was going?"

"I think he said he was going to St. Paul. I made a suit of clothes for him in a great hurry, as he was very anxious to get away."

"What kind of a suit did he get?" asked Manning, now anxious to learn the clothing of the man, in order that he might the more accurately describe him.

"It was from this piece," said Mr. Griswold, throwing on the table a roll of dark green cassimere. "That is one of the latest importations, and as fine a piece of goods as I have in the house."

"I like that myself," said the detective. "Would you object to giving me a small piece of it as a sample? I want to show it to a friend of mine at the hotel, who has pretty good taste in such matters."

"Of course not," replied Mr. Griswold, as he clipped off a piece of the cloth, little dreaming of the use to which the detective would put it.

Declining to make a selection until he had sought the advice of an imaginary friend, and stating that he would probably call again in the evening, Manning took his leave of the little tailor. The detective then repaired to the railroad ticket office, where he had a friend of long standing, from whom he hoped to derive some material information.

At the railroad station he found his friend on duty, and after the usual friendly salutations, he requested a few moments' private conversation. Being admitted to an inner office, Manning at once displayed the photograph of Duncan, and asked:

"Harry, have you seen that face about here, say within about two weeks?"

Taking the picture, and regarding it intently for a moment, he said:

"Why, yes – that's Duncan from Des Moines. I know him very well. He has been here often."

"Well, has he been here within two weeks?"

"Yes, he was here about two weeks ago on a spree, and he bought a ticket for St. Paul."

"Are you quite sure about that?"

"Perfectly sure," answered the ticket agent. "I remember it distinctly, and what impressed it the more forcibly upon my mind is the fact that he wanted to know if I could give him a ticket on the Northern Pacific road from here, and I told him he would have to go to St. Paul for that."

"Did he mention any particular point on the railroad that he wanted a ticket for?" asked Manning.

"No, I think not. He simply said he was making for Dakota."

Ascertaining that a train would leave for St. Paul in an hour, the detective purchased a ticket for that city, and thanking the agent for his information, he returned to the hotel to make arrangements for continuing his journey. Before leaving, however, he telegraphed me his destination, and what he had been able to learn.

From this information it was evident that Duncan was endeavoring to reach the far west, and there seek a refuge among some of the numerous mining camps which abound in that section of the country, hoping by that means to successfully elude pursuit, should any be made for him. It was plainly evident to me that he was entirely unaware of being followed, and, in fact, of anything that had taken place since the robbery, and that he was simply following his own blind inclinations to hide himself as effectually as he could.

The first task performed by Manning after reaching St. Paul, was to examine all the hotel registers, in the hope of discovering some traces of an entry resembling the peculiar handwriting of Duncan. He also took the precaution to quietly display the photograph of the young man to all the clerks of the various hostelries, trusting that someone would recognize him as one who had been their guest on some previous occasion. In this, too, he was disappointed. Among the many to whom he displayed Duncan's picture, not one of them had any recollection of such an individual.

Feeling somewhat disheartened at this non-success, Manning next sought the chief of police, and enlisted his services in our behalf. That evening, in company with an officer, he made a tour among the houses of ill repute, and here, too, disappointment awaited him. Not one among the number whom he approached had any knowledge of the man, and therefore could give him no information.

Tired and puzzled and vexed, he at length was compelled to return to the hotel, and seek his much-needed repose.

His experience in St. Paul had thus far been far from satisfactory, and yet the thought of abandoning his investigations in that city never occurred to him. He had too frequently been compelled to battle with unpromising circumstances in the past, to allow a temporary discomfiture to dishearten him now. He felt that he was upon the right track, that Duncan had certainly come from Sioux City to St. Paul, but whether he had remained here any length of time, or had pushed on without stopping, was the question that bothered him immensely. Resolving, therefore, to renew his efforts in the morning, he soon fell asleep.

On the morrow, when he descended to the office of the hotel, preparatory to partaking of his morning repast, he noticed with some little surprise that a new face was behind the counter.

Surmising that this might be the night clerk, yet unrelieved from his duties, and that Duncan might have arrived during the time he officiated, Manning approached him, and propounded the usual question. When he brought forth the photograph, to his intense delight, the clerk recognized it at once. Turning to the register and hastily running over the leaves, he pointed to a name inscribed thereon.

"That's the man," said he confidently.

Manning looked at the name indicated, and found scrawled in a very uncertain hand:

"John Tracy, Denver, Col."

"He came in on a night train," continued the clerk. "He only remained to breakfast and went away shortly afterward."

"Have you any idea which way he went?" inquired Manning.

"No, I cannot tell you that. He left the hotel shortly after breakfast in a hack. He did not return after that, but sent the hackman here to pay his bill and to obtain his valise. He acted very strange while he was here, and I felt somewhat suspicious of him."

"Can you tell me the name of this hackman?" now asked Manning.

"I think his name is Davids," answered the clerk, "but I will ask the baggage-man about him; he can, no doubt, tell me who he is."

The baggage-man was summoned and he distinctly remembered the occurrence, and that the driver's name was Billy Davids, who was well-known throughout the city, particularly among the sporting fraternity.

Thanking both of these men for the information which they had given him, the detective, forgetting all about his breakfast, hastened to the office of the chief of police, and acquainting him with what he had heard, expressed his desire to see this hackman at once.

The chief, who knew the man, at once volunteered to accompany him, and they left the office together in search of the important cab-driver. It being yet quite early in the morning, they went directly to the stable, and here they found Billy Davids in the act of harnessing his horses and preparing for his day's work.

"Good morning, Billy," said the chief, good-naturedly. "You are making an early start, I see; are you busy?"

"No, sir," answered Mr. Davids; "I can take you gentlemen wherever you want to go."

"Not today, Billy; but I have a friend here who wants to talk to you, and you may find it to your interest to tell him what he wishes to know."

Manning stepped forward and stated, in as few words as possible, what he desired, and at length displayed the inevitable photograph.

Davids recognized it at once, as a "party" who had engaged him to take himself and a woman from the hotel, to a resort some distance from the city, known as the "Halfway House." He performed this duty, and later in the day, after waiting several hours, the man had given him ten dollars and sent him back to the hotel to pay his bill and to obtain his valise. After performing this service, he returned to the Halfway House, and waited there until dark, when Duncan came out alone, and was driven to the Northern Pacific depot. Arriving here, he paid the hackman quite liberally and dismissed him, saying that he was going to leave town on the next train westward.

"Have you any idea where he was going?" asked Manning.

"I think he went to Minneapolis, for he asked me if that road would take him there, and I saw him get aboard the train for that city;" answered the driver.

This was all that Davids could tell; and after remunerating him for his trouble, Manning left him to finish his preparations for the day.

Here was the very information he wanted, and he had struck the trail again. Anxious to pursue his journey, Manning invited the chief to breakfast with him; after which, finding he could leave in a very short time, he bade the courteous and valuable officer good-bye, and was soon on his way to Minneapolis, there to commence again the trail of the fleeing burglar.

Chapter XVIII

The Detective at Bismarck — Further Traces of the Fugitive — A Protracted Orgy — A Jewish Friend of the Burglar in Trouble.

On arriving in Minneapolis, Manning was able to discover without serious difficulty that Duncan, after remaining in that city two days, had purchased a ticket over the Northern Pacific railroad for Bismarck, a thriving town in Dakota. This information he had been able to gain by a resort to his old method of visiting the houses of ill-fame, and then carelessly exposing Duncan's photograph to the various inmates, in such a manner as to excite no suspicion of his real errand. His experience thus far had been that Duncan, either to evade pursuit, to gratify bestial passion, or to endeavor by such excitements to drive away the haunting fear that oppressed him, had invariably sought the companionship of the harlot and the profligate. Being possessed of plenty of money, it may be imagined that he experienced no difficulty in finding associates willing to minister to his appetites, and to assist him in forgetting the dangers that threatened him, by dissipation and debauchery. All along his path were strewn these evidences of reckless abandonment, which, while they temporarily enabled him to drown the remembrances of his crime, yet, at the same time, they served most powerfully to point out to his pursuer the road he was traveling.

It appeared, therefore, that my first theories were correct, and that Thomas Duncan was making his way to the far western country, where, beyond the easy and expeditious mode of communication by railroad and telegraph, he would be safe from pursuit. He was evidently seeking to reach the mining district, where, among men as reckless as himself, he hoped to evade the officers of law.

Manning lost no time in following up the clew he had obtained in Minneapolis, and so, purchasing a ticket for Bismarck, he was soon thundering on his way to the Missouri river. At Brainerd, at Fargo in Minnesota, and at Jamestown in Dakota, during the time when the train had stopped for some necessary purpose, he had made inquiries, and at each place was rewarded by gleaning some information, however fragmentary, of the fugitive. He was therefore assured that he was upon the trail, and that unless something unforeseen occurred, he would sooner or later overtake the object of his pursuit.

On the following day Manning arrived at Bismarck, a thrifty and growing little town on the banks of the muddy Missouri. As the train left the more thickly populated country and emerged into the region of this as yet comparatively undeveloped west, the detective was surprised to witness the rapid advancements that had been made within a few years. The spirit of American energy and enterprise was reaching out into this vast region, and already the influences of modern civilization and thrift were manifesting themselves. No longer a trackless waste, abandoned to the roaming bands of Indians and the wild beasts of the forest, and plain, the western continent was fast yielding to the plowshare of the husbandman, and to the powerful agencies of education and improvement.

Bismarck itself was a wonderfully active town, and during the season of navigation a large commercial business was transacted with the various towns upon the river, both above and below it. Before the advent of the Northern Pacific railroad, Bismarck had an existence, but simply as a sleepy river station, with its periodical bursts of life and animation during the months when the river was navigable and when trade along its waters was possible. When winter came, however, with its chilling blasts, and the river was frozen, trade almost ceased entirely, and Bismarck remained in sluggish inactivity until spring with its refreshing showers and balmy breezes awakened it to new life and being. Now, however, all was changed. The railroad with its facilities, had opened the way to emigration; the pioneers had penetrated the solitudes, and Bismarck had grown with that wonderful rapidity so characteristic of the western town. The advent of the iron horse had opened up new and hitherto undreamed of possibilities. Real estate, which had previously no fixed value whatever, was now in demand at almost fabulous prices. Stores and dwellings sprang into being, hotels and churches were built, school houses and even banking institutions flourished with a vigor that seemed almost miraculous.

Sauntering about the town on the morning after his arrival, Manning was surprised at the activity and bustle, the thrift and energy which greeted him on every hand. His past experiences had taught him many things which he found of use to him in making his inquiries in Bismarck, and it was not long before he succeeded in learning definite particulars of Duncan's stay in this place. From reliable sources he ascertained that the young man had arrived in the town about two weeks prior to this, and had remained several days, enjoying himself in much the same manner that had marked his residence in the other cities along his route, except that in Bismarck he had exposed himself to a greater extent than at any other place. It seemed that as he got further west, his fears of pursuit and detection grew less, and he became more bold and open in his actions. Here he had not attempted concealment at all, except as to his name, which he gave as Tom Moore, of Chicago; his carousals were publicly known, and the lavish expenditure of his stolen money was commented upon by many.

In a conversation with the proprietor of the hotel at which Duncan had stopped, the detective learned that his stay in the city had been marked by the most reckless dissipation and extravagance. So careless did he appear in the display of his money, of which he appeared to have a large amount, that the proprietor had taken it upon himself to warn him against the danger to which such a course would expose him. The town was infested with a gang of roughs and thieves, and he feared that if once they became aware of Duncan's wealth, his life would be of comparatively little value. Several of these characters had been seen about the hotel, and the landlord had remonstrated seriously with Duncan about his folly. To this Duncan had impudently replied that he could take care of himself, and needed no advice. Finding it of no use, therefore, to advise him, the landlord desisted in his efforts, and left him to follow his own inclinations.

Manning also learned from his host that Duncan had associated quite intimately while in the city, with a Jew clothing merchant, who was a resident here, and who seemed to be an old acquaintance. The name of this man was Jacob Gross, and ascertaining where his place of business was located, Manning determined to give him a call.

When he entered the store of Mr. Gross, that gentleman was engaged in waiting upon a customer. He was a perfect type of the Israelite — sharp-featured, with prominent nose, keen, glittering eyes and curly black hair. If any doubt of his race remained, the manner in which he conducted his bargain with his unsuspecting customer would have convinced anyone of the presence of the veritable Jew.

Manning watched, with amused interest, the tact with which the Hebrew clothier endeavored to convince his customer that a coat, much too large for him, was "yust a fit and no mistake," and that the price which he asked was not half as much as the garment was worth.

After the customer had departed, the clothier advanced, bowing and smiling, toward the detective, as if anticipating another sale as profitable as the last one. Manning informed him in a few words that he was looking for Duncan, and was a friend of his, who was desirous of gaining some information of his present whereabouts, as unless he saw him, Duncan might be getting into more trouble.

It appeared that Duncan had told the same gambling story to Mr. Gross, who seemed to be dreadfully shocked at the affair.

"Py gracious," said he excitedly, "I hafe knowed dot boy ven I sold cloding in Des Moines, more as fife years ago, and so help me Moses I did nefer belief he vud do such a ting loike dot."

After further conversation, he learned that Duncan had spent a great deal of his time at this store, and when he left, had stated that he intended to go on to Miles City, and perhaps to Butte City, Montana. It appeared that Duncan had an uncle who was engaged in the clothing business at Butte City, and that it was possible he might eventually get there.

"If you find him," said Mr. Gross, after he had given the above information, "you musn't told him where you heard this, because he told me, I should say nothing about him to anybody."

"All right," replied Manning, "if I find him, it won't make much difference to him who told me about him."

As he uttered these words a peculiar look came into the shrewd face of the Jew, a look which was partly of quick suspicion and of fear, and he eyed the imperturbable detective for a few moments as though seriously in doubt about the whole affair. Manning, however, had nothing further to say, and bidding the clothier a pleasant farewell he left the store.

On returning to the hotel, he found that he had several hours to wait, as no train would leave Bismarck until evening, and he therefore employed his time in writing up his reports and mailing them to me.

After partaking of an early tea, he returned to the railroad station, where he discovered that he had yet some time to wait before the arrival of the train, which was belated. As he was standing on the rude platform, musing over the events which had taken place in his journey thus far, and speculating as to the probable result of his chase after an individual who had seemed, phantomlike, to have eluded his grasp at every point.

He knew full well the desperation of the man he was following, and the threat that "no two men should take him alive," was, he realized, no idle one. He had no doubt that unless he could circumvent him in some way, his capture might be no easy task, and that in this undeveloped country he was taking his life in his hands in the journey he was now making. He never faltered for an instant, however; he was determined to capture this criminal, if possible, and he quietly murmured to himself: "Well, let the worst come, a quick eye and a steady hand are good things to have in a meeting like this may be, and I'll take care that Thomas Duncan does not catch me napping."

His meditations were suddenly interrupted by the unexpected appearance of the little Jewish tailor, who, breathless and panting, now came scrambling up on the platform and exclaimed:

"Py gracious, Mr. Manning! I vas afraid you vas gone, and I hafe somedings on my mindt dot bodders me like de dickens!"

"What is it that troubles you, Mr. Gross?" inquired the detective, laughing in spite of himself at the little fellow's distress.

"Vell, I'll told you," he answered, mopping the perspiration which was streaming from his face. "I was tinkin' dot may be if you git dot fellow, you vould be vantin' me for a vitness, and s'help me Moses I vould not do dot — not for dwo hundred tollar."

"Oh, you need not give yourself any uneasiness on that score, Mr. Gross," said Manning; "you will not be wanted in any case whatever."

"My gootness, I vas glad of dot. If I vas to leaf my bisness I vould be ruined. Dot's all right, dough. Let's go und take a glass of peer."

At this juncture, the shrill whistle of the approaching train was heard, and this fact enabled the detective to decline the proffered beverage. After a hearty hand-shake from the nervous little clothier, Manning sprang upon the train and in a few moments later he was on his way to Miles City.

Chapter XIX

From Bismarck to Bozeman — The Trail Growing Warmer — Duncan Buys a Pony — A Long Stage Ride.

*T*he distance from Bismarck to Miles City is about three hundred miles, and as Manning left the former place early in the evening, he secured a couch in the comfortable sleeping car, and shortly afterward retired to rest. It seemed almost incredible the giant strides which had been made in a few years in the process of civilization in our western country. But yesterday the ground which our operative was now traveling in comfort, was overrun by the Indian and the wild beasts of the forest, and today along his entire route were rising up substantial towns and villages, bringing in their wake the enlightening influences of education and morality. The railroad, that mighty agent of civilization, is rapidly forging a chain of communication between the two great oceans, and travel in the western wilds, formerly fraught with hardships and dangers unspeakable, is now performed with rapidity, comfort and safety. In the morning the train stopped at Little Missouri, where the passengers were refreshed with breakfast, then on again past Sentinel Butte, they left the boundaries of Dakota and entered the great territory of Montana. On again like the rush of the wind, until about five o'clock in the afternoon, they arrived at Miles City, where the train was to remain nearly two hours, before continuing their journey.

Miles City was another striking illustration of the wonderful growth of American towns. Less than a year ago, a barren waste marked the spot where now was growing a thriving city. The railroad, as in other localities, had played an important part in awakening this uninhabited region to life and activity. The trackless, boundless prairie had been reclaimed, and was now a flourishing city, full of bustle and vigor. Making his way to a neat and comfortable hotel, which bore the rather euphonious title of St. Cloud, Manning partook of a substantial meal and then set about his investigations. He soon found news of the object of his inquiries. From the proprietor of the St. Cloud, he learned that Duncan had remained here two days, and upon the register he saw the now well-known signature of Tom Moore of Chicago. He had informed the inn-keeper of his intention of going to Bozeman, a town lying to the north of the Crow Reservation.

Manning resolved, therefore, to press right on, and he returned to the railroad station, where the train was still waiting. Purchasing a ticket for Billings, he started again on his way, and at nearly midnight he arrived at his destination, where he secured quarters for the night.

Billings was, at this time, the terminal point of the Northern Pacific railroad, and as the detective sought the open air on the following morning, he was amazed at the scenes that were presented to his view. The place was literally swarming with people. Prospectors, land-buyers, traders, merchants, and a miscellaneous army of railroad men were everywhere. No time had been afforded in which to build suitable structures for housing the ever-increasing population, and the town presented the appearance of a huge encampment; nearly one-half of the city being composed of canvas tents. In the hotels, on the corners of the streets, and in the places of business, the universal topic of conversation was the phenomenal growth of the city, and the grand prospects which the future had in store for this embryonic western metropolis. Along the railroad, a perfect army of workmen were assembled, awaiting their orders for the day. Graders, tie-men, track-layers and construction corps, were already on the spot, and they too seemed imbued with the same spirit of enthusiasm which filled their more wealthy and ambitious neighbors in the city. As may readily be imagined, crime and immorality followed hand in hand with the march of improvement. The gambler and the harlot plied their vocations in the full light of day, and as yet unrebuked by the ruling powers of a community, too newly located to assume the dignity of enacting laws.

The detective made his way through the streets, mentally noting these things, while his efforts were directed to finding some trace of Thomas Duncan. He made a systematic tour of the hotels, or more properly speaking, the boarding-houses with which the town was filled, and after numerous disappointments, was at last successful in learning something definite of the movements of his man. At a hotel called the "Windsor," he found the unmistakable signature he was looking for, and was convinced that Tom Moore of Chicago had preceded him but a few days. Exhibiting his talismanic photograph to the proprietor, he was informed that Duncan had been there some ten days before, and after remaining a day or two, had gone over to the military cantonments, some four or five miles distant, where a detachment of United States soldiers were quartered.

Procuring a horse, Manning started for the cantonment, where he was kindly received by Major Bell, the officer in charge, who informed him that Duncan had been there some days before, and that he had remained about the camp for several days, playing cards with the soldiers and enjoying himself generally. During his stay he had purchased a pony from a Crow Indian, and while he was at the cantonment he rode into Billings and bought a Sharp's repeating rifle, after which he had mounted his horse and rode off in the direction of Fort Custer. He had remained away several days when he again returned to the cantonment, and after remaining there one night, he had started on horseback for Bozeman and Helena.

This was authentic and gratifying intelligence. Manning had received not only reliable information as to the movements of Duncan, but the distance between them had been materially lessened by the fugitive's long detention at the cantonment. The burglar was now but a few days ahead of him, and if nothing transpired to delay him, he would soon overtake the man, who, from all indications, was entirely unsuspicious of the fact that a detective was upon his track who had followed his trail as closely and as unerringly as the Indian follows the track of the beast through forest and stream. As an additional means of identification, Manning secured a full description of the horse purchased by Duncan, and with this increased fund of information, Manning returned to Billings. On the following morning, seated beside the driver on the top of the stagecoach, and behind four dashing bay horses, Manning rattled out of the pushing little town of Billings on his way to Bozeman.

He now indulged in high hopes of soon overhauling Duncan, and all along their way, whenever the stage stopped to change horses, he was gratified to receive the information that the man and the pony which he described had passed over the same route a few days in advance of him.

The road from Billings to Bozeman led them part of the distance along the Yellowstone river, and through a country wild and picturesque in the extreme. Sometimes winding around the sides of a huge mountain, from which they obtained a magnificent view of the rugged and beautiful scenery below, and again descending to the valleys, they swept along between the mountains which towered aloft on either hand, their rugged sides forming a marked contrast with the emerald-hued verdure skirting their base. Occasional ranches presented the evidences of cultivation and profitable stock-raising. Broad fields and luxuriant pastures were spread before the view, and hundreds of sleek cattle were scattered over the country, either sleeping quietly in the sun or browsing upon the rich, tender herbage which abounds. At these ranches the horses were frequently changed, and the mail was delivered, much to the gratification of these hardy pioneers, who were otherwise shut out from the busy actions of the world beyond them.

The country through which they passed was exceedingly rich in an agricultural point of view, the resources of which cannot be overestimated, and the atmosphere was dry and pure. Inhaling the invigorating air as they rode along, Manning suffered none of the discomforts which are naturally consequent upon a journey by stage of more than one hundred and fifty miles. At noon, they stopped at a ranch station, and here they were regaled with a repast which would have tickled the palate of an epicure. Broiled trout from a mountain stream near by, roast fowl and a variety of dishes, made up a feast well worthy of the lusty appetites of the travelers. Here, too, Manning received tidings of the fleeing burglar. His horse, which was a fine one, and peculiarly marked, had been noticed particularly by the ranchmen, so there was no doubt that he was upon the right road to overtake him.

After the dinner, and a good resting spell, they resumed their journey. Now their road ran along the fertile valley, and again passing through a sharp defile in the mountains, and finally winding its way along a narrow ledge of rock, where the slightest turn to left or right, a single misstep of the sure-footed animals, or an awkward move of their driver, would have hurled them into an abyss hundreds of feet below, where instant and horrible death awaited them.

No accident befell them, however, and just as the sun was going down in a blaze of glory, behind the towering mountains into the west, they arrived at a ranch for supper and rest.

In the evening the moon came out, illuminating the landscape with a soft enchanting beauty, as its beams fell upon the tall mountain and the level plain, lighting up tree and flower, and flashing upon the river like a myriad of polished gems. As they rode along, song and story enlivened the journey, and a draft or two from a wicker-covered flask which the detective carried, soon produced an era of good feeling between the outside passengers and the burly, good-natured driver.

"Have you ever been bothered with robbers or highwaymen along this route?" asked Manning of their driver during a lull in the conversation.

"Well, we used to be," answered the fat fellow, with a quiet chuckle, as he cracked his whip unpleasantly near to the flank of the off leader, who was lagging a little; "but of late we haven't seen anything of the kind."

"Ever had any adventure with them yourself?" asked Manning in a coaxing tone, as he fancied he could see that the old fellow had a story which he could be induced to relate.

"Yes," he answered, puffing quietly away at a cigar which Manning had given him. "About a year ago I had a little experience up near Thompson's place, which we will reach about ten o'clock, if we have no bad luck."

"Let us hear it, won't you?" asked one of the other passengers, now becoming interested.

"Well," answered the driver, evidently pleased at finding himself an object of interest, "wait until we round this spur here, and then we'll have a tolerable straight road ahead. I don't suppose, though, that you'll find it very interesting."

In a few moments they passed around the spur of the mountain, and the whole landscape was lighted up with a blaze of moonlight that flooded the scene with a radiance beautiful to behold. No living habitation was within sight, and the rumble of the coach was the only sound that broke the stillness that brooded over the scene.

The driver settled himself back in his seat, and after a few preparatory coughs, and a swallow of brandy, to clear his throat, began his narration.

Chapter XX

The Stage Driver's Story.

"Well," said the driver, as he set his long-lashed whip into its socket, and gathered up his reins in his left hand, in order to afford him an opportunity to declaim more freely with his right, "you must know that I've been drivin' on this line more than two years, and consequently I know every inch of the route like a book. I must own, though, that I didn't know quite as much at the time I speak of. The driver whose place I took when I came on to the road, had been pretty badly used up in a scrimmage with the bandits about a week before, and I didn't like the prospects, you may be sure; but as I was out of a job, I took this, and I made up my mind when I commenced, never to put my head in the way of a robber's bullet, if I could help it."

"That's the case with most of you, isn't it?" said Manning, good-naturedly.

"What makes you think so?" inquired the driver, quizzically.

"Why, the ease and success with which stagecoaches have usually been robbed," was the reply.

"Well, I'll tell you," he answered, good-humoredly, and not the least disturbed by Manning's quiet reflection on the bravery of stage drivers in general. "When a fellow has to manage four tolerably skittish horses with both hands full of leather, he haint much time to fool around huntin' shootin' irons, 'specially when he's got to look down into the muzzle of a repeater which is likely to go off and hurt somebody."

"Do you think these stage robbers, as a rule, are disposed to kill anybody?" asked Manning.

"Why, sir," answered the driver, "they would just as soon kill a stage driver as eat their breakfast, and they know how to handle a rifle, too, let me tell you."

"There's something in that reasoning," replied Manning, laughingly. "But go on with your story."

"Well," continued the driver, "I had made several trips and had met with no trouble or accident, so I began to think the gang had gone away from these parts, and that there was no danger to be feared. However, I still carried a brace of good revolvers in a handy place, just to make sure I was safe; though, Lord bless you, I knew I couldn't get at them in time to do any good, if the robbers did attack us.

"Well, one morning — it was a cold, raw day in April — I left Billings with my coach full of people, most of whom were goin' through to Helena, although I only drove as far as Bozeman, just as I do now. I had nine passengers, all told, and among the number was an old ranchman named Kyle Barton, and his handsome daughter. I tell you, she was a stunner; her hair was as black as a crow, and her bright black eyes sparkled like diamonds. I knew 'em both pretty well, for the old man owned a ranch out near Bozeman, and was as fine a man as ever stood six feet in his boots. The young woman was a fiery little beauty, and as hard to manage as a three-year-old colt. The old man and his daughter had been on a trip to the East, and were now returning home again, after bein' away several months. Well, the young woman, as I have said, for all she was as pretty as a picture, had a devilish wicked look in her flashing black eyes, that made a fellow kind 'o wilt when she looked him square in the face.

"The young woman took her seat on the inside, while the old man, who was hardy and tough as a pine knot, took his place on the outside, right where you are sittin' now. It was pretty cold, and we had to bundle up pretty well, but the old man didn't mind it a bit. He smoked his pipe and passed his bottle — thankee', yes, sir, I don't care if I do — and we were enjoying of ourselves amazin'.

"We journeyed along all day," continued the driver, as he handed the bottle back, and wiped his lips with the sleeve of his coat, "and nothin' happened to hinder or delay us in the least. Instead of gittin' warmer as the day wore on, it kept gittin' a dern sight colder, until along about four o'clock in the afternoon, when it began to snow, and by early dark, it was hard at it, a regular December snowstorm, with a drivin' wind that cut our faces tremendous. This bothered us a good deal, for the snow being wet and sticky, would ball up on the horses' feet so that they could hardly stand, and we just poked along our way at a gait not a bit faster than a slow walk. We couldn't get along any faster, and it was no use a-beatin' the poor critters, for they was a-doin' all in their power, and a-strainin' every nerve to keep a-movin'.

"The old ranchman was a good-hearted, sociable old fellow, and he didn't seem to mind the storm a bit. As we plodded along he talked about his cattle ranch, the price of cattle, and what profit he had made that year. It was along after dinner, and we had both been strikin' the bottle pretty regular, although the cold was so great we could hardly feel it, when he fell to talkin' about himself and his daughter. We were the only two outside, and he became quite confidential like, and I pitied the old man, for he'd had a deal of trouble with the young spitfire inside.

"Among other things, he told me that she had almost broken his old heart lately by fallin' in love, or imaginin' she had, with one of his herdsmen, a handsome, dashing, devil-may-care sort of a fellow he had picked up at Bozeman and taken out to his ranch about a year before. When the old man found out that the gal was gone on the fellow, and that he was a-meetin' her after dark, he ups and discharges him instanter, and gives him a piece of his mind about his takin' a mean advantage of the confidence which had been placed in him.

"His daughter, Stella, as he called her, fought against his dischargin' of the young man, and had been sullen and ill-tempered ever since her lover left. He had caught them correspondin' with each other after that, and on one occasion he was certain they had a clandestine meetin'. On findin' out that his daughter was determined not to give up this worthless young cuss, the old man made up his mind to take her away, and he had accordin'ly packed up and gone on a long journey to the East, where he had stayed several months, and they were now just gettin' back to their home again. The old man had hoped that absence from her lover and meetin' with other people in different scenes, would induce her to forget her old passion, and to realize the folly she had committed in seekin' to marry such a worthless fellow against her father's wishes."

"I don't see what this has got to do with the bandits, though," now said the detective, who was getting a little anxious to find out what all this was leading to.

"I was afraid it wouldn't interest you much," replied the driver; "but you'll soon see the point to my story and what this young girl had to do with it."

"I beg your pardon," said Manning, "I am interested in it, only I was anxious to hear where the bandits came in. Let's take a little drop of brandy, and I promise you I won't interrupt you again until you have finished."

Here he handed the flask over to the old man, who took it with the remark that it "looked for all the world like the one carried by the old ranchman," and after a hearty pull at it, passed it back again, and resumed his story.

"As the darkness increased, the old ranchman, who it seemed had heard of the recent robberies, began to grow a little nervous, although he didn't appear to be a dern bit scared. He looked carefully to the condition of his pistols, and also advised me to have mine handy in case of need; nothin' would satisfy him but I had to get mine out of the box, and after he had looked them all over, they were laid on the seat between us. Not content with this, he warned the inside passengers that there was danger to be apprehended, and that there were bandits on the road. He urged them to have their weapons in readiness, so that in case the robbers did come, we could give them a red-hot reception. The people inside caught the old man's spirit, and they all resolved that if an attack did come they would meet it like men. To tell the truth, I didn't fear any danger, and I thought the old man was excitin' everybody without cause; but I didn't say anything, cause it wouldn't do any harm anyhow, even if we were not molested.

"However, I had reckoned without my host, for just as we reached this place, and were a-turnin' around this bend in the road, two men sprang out from the bushes and grabbed the lead horses by the bits. Two more jumped out on one side of the coach, and two more on the other, while one man stepped up to me and demanded me to come down. Of course the coach was stopped, and just as the robber spoke to me, the old man reached over in front of me and fired. The robber fell at once without a sound. Barton then fired at the man at the horse's head nearest him, and brought him down. These shots were both fired as quick as a flash, but his aim had been unerring. 'Duck down, Davy, duck down,' he cried to me as he swung himself from the coach, and a volley of bullets passed over our heads.

"I followed his example, and in a hurry, too, and escaped unhurt. Just then we heard two reports from the passengers inside, and in less time that it has taken me to tell it the scrimmage was over and the robbers who were unhurt had fled, leaving three of their number on the ground, two of them seriously wounded, and the other one as dead as a post, with a bullet hole plum through his forehead.

"As soon as they could the passengers clambered out of the coach, and by the aid of our lanterns, we found the robbers as I have just told you. We all congratulated ourselves on our fortunate escape, and the old man was warmly commended for his forethought and for the gallant service he had rendered.

"I saw the old man did not seem disposed to say much, but I also noticed a look of grim satisfaction on his face as he looked down at the dead bandit. He then looked anxiously toward the coach, and seemed relieved to find that his daughter still remained inside.

"We bound up as well as we could the wounds of the other two, and lifted them to the top of the coach. When it came to the dead one, some of the passengers were in favor of lettin' him lie where he was, but others objected and wanted to take him along with us, as we did not have far to go."

"While we were discussin' the question, the young woman, who had got out of the coach while we were talkin', and without her father observin' her, caught sight of the bandit's face, as he lay on his back in the snow, and with a wild scream of anguish, she pushed the men aside and flung herself upon the lifeless body. Her sobs were terrible to hear, and many a strong man turned away to hide the tears that came to their eyes in spite of them. Her father approached her and tried to draw her away, but all to no use, until at length her strength gave out, and she fainted dead away.

"You see," continued the driver, "that dead man was her lover. He had been engaged in the business of robbin' stagecoaches for a long time, and only hired with the old man as a cover to hide his real business, and to try and win the girl, whom he had frequently seen before.

"The old man was all broke up about the girl, but he was glad that things had happened as they did, and he felt sure that after her grief was over, she would not fail to see the danger she had escaped, and to thank her father for savin' her from a life of shame and disgrace.

"We lifted the girl into the coach, and put the dead man along with the others on the top. He had been the terror of the neighborhood, although no one knew, until this time, who had been the leader of this murderous gang. We buried him at Bozeman, and since that time we have had no trouble with anything like bandits or robbers along the route."

"What became of the other two?" asked the detective.

"They were put under arrest, but somehow they managed to escape before they were brought to trial, and that was the last we ever heard of them."

"And the girl," asked Manning, "what became of her?"

"Oh, she is all right now; as pert as a cricket, and prettier than ever," answered the driver. "She was married some time ago to a young fellow who is the sheriff of the county here, and is as happy as the day is long. You wouldn't know that she ever had an experience like this, and I don't believe she ever thinks of her bandit lover, while she hangs around her old father with all the affection of a child, and the old ranchman is as happy and contented a man as you will find in the whole county."

As the driver concluded his narrative, the stage rolled into Bozeman, and at sharp midnight they drew up before the door of the inn. The moon was still shining, and lights were flashing from the windows when they arrived. Tired and hungry, the passengers alighted, and after a light lunch, Manning procured a bed and retired to rest.

Chapter XXI

False Information which Nearly Proves Fatal — A Night Ride to Helena — Dangers by the Wayside.

Traveling by coach is far from being as comfortable and pleasant as a journey by rail. The time occupied in going comparatively short distances is very great, besides the rough jolting over uneven roads which is a natural concomitant of stagecoach travel. It is true that by the easy locomotion of a journey of this kind, a much better view of the surrounding country is afforded, and the traveler finds ample opportunities to admire the beauty of nature everywhere spread before him; but even that palls upon the eye when the journey is protracted from early morn until midnight, and the traveler is cramped up in an uncomfortable position upon the driver's box. Under such circumstances, after a time, there is but little compensation for the trials and fatigues of a journey such as Manning had just completed when he arrived at Bozeman on the night before. The road through which they had come led them through a country so varied in its grand and imposing beauty, towering rocks and fertile valleys, winding streams and gentle elevations, that for a time fatigue was forgotten in the enjoyment of the scenes about him, and it was not until the journey had been completed that he realized how utterly wearied and tired out he was. His limbs were sore and stiffened from his cramped position, and being unable to sleep at all on the journey, he was completely exhausted when he sought his couch at the hotel at Bozeman. Being of a strong and healthy physique, however, and upheld by an ambition to succeed in the mission he had undertaken, Manning arose in the morning, and after a refreshing bath and an excellent breakfast, was quite rested and fully prepared to continue his efforts.

Bozeman, unlike the other towns which he had passed through upon his journey, was remotely situated as yet from railroad communication, and yet in spite of that fact was a busy and well-populated little town. It is the county seat of Gallatin county, and contained at this time several pretentious stores, a hotel, a national bank, and a goodly number of substantial dwellings. As may naturally be inferred, there was the usual complement of saloons, in which drinking and gambling were indulged in without license, and with no fear of restraint from the prohibitory influences of the law.

Failing to find any trace of Thomas Duncan, or "Tom Moore," at the hotel, Manning began his usual systematic tour of these houses of public entertainment. House after house was visited, and the day waned without his making the slightest discovery that would avail him at all in his pursuit. At length, however, as night was falling, he encountered a saloon-keeper, who in answer to his inquiries gruffly informed him, that a person answering Duncan's description and mounted upon a pony resembling his, had stopped in his saloon a few days before, and had gone away in the direction of the Yellowstone Park.

This was rather disappointing intelligence, for it required him to retrace his steps, and go back over ground which he had already traveled. However, if the information was reliable, no time was to be lost, and he started from the saloon to commence his preparations at once.

While at the bar, he had noticed a sturdy, honest-looking miner, who was taking a drink, and who had stopped and looked intently at him while the proprietor had given him the information above mentioned. As Manning left the saloon, the man followed him a short distance, and when out of sight of the saloon called after him; Manning stopped and the man came toward him.

"Mister," said he, as he approached the detective, "ef ye go to the park, you won't find the man yer arter, that's a dead sure thing."

"What do you mean?" asked Manning with some surprise.

"I means as how the boss of the saloon yonder has lied to ye, that's all."

"What makes you think so?"

"Bekase I passed the man ye wor askin' about three days ago, on the road to Helena."

"Are you sure about this?"

"Well, I reckon I am. I couldn't make much of a mistake about that white-faced pony he wor a-ridin'."

Requesting the miner to accompany him to the hotel, Manning interrogated him closely about the appearance of the man, and found that he was giving him the correct information, as his description of Duncan tallied precisely with what he himself had already learned. After carefully weighing the matter, Manning decided to act upon this latter information, and to start for Helena that evening. The saloon-keeper evidently mistrusted some danger to Duncan, from the detective's inquiries, and Manning was inclined to believe that the fugitive had stopped there during his stay in Bozeman, and that the proprietor of the saloon had attempted to deceive him and turn him off from the tracks of the unfortunate burglar.

Thus far, from all that could be learned of Duncan's movements, the young man was traveling entirely alone. From point to point across the western continent Manning had traced him, and no tidings of a companion had been as yet received. Alone and friendless, cut off from all the old associations of his past life, this unfortunate man was flying from a fate which he felt must be impending. Through the long summer days and under the starry skies during the weary nights, this fleeing outcast was working his way to fancied freedom and security. I wonder if, during the long watches of the night, when he sought the needed slumber which his weary brain and body demanded, whether the accuser's voice was not sounding in his ears, whether he did not start with affright at fancied dangers, and find his lonely life a burden, heavy and sorrowful!

It was now nearly eight o'clock, and the stage would not leave for Helena until midnight, and Manning, having nothing else to do, sought a few hours' sleep in order to be better prepared for the long journey before him. The distance from Bozeman to Helena was about ninety-five miles, and from what he had heard the roads were in a terrible condition. Heavy rains had fallen recently, and the mud in some places along his journey was said to be nearly axle deep. Undaunted by the gloomy prospect before him, however, Manning rested quietly, and, when the time for starting arrived, he was fully refreshed and eager for the long ride before him.

Profiting by his past experience, he now secured an inside seat, as he would be better protected from the chilling night winds so prevalent in this mountainous country, and would perhaps, be able to sleep at intervals during the hours which would ensue before daylight.

The other passengers in the coach were three men who were interested in mining in the neighborhood of Helena, and who, like himself, were bound for that place. They were all, however, rather wearied with their journey from Billings, and very much disposed to sleep. Manning, therefore, stowed himself away in one corner of the coach, as comfortably as he was able to do, and nodded and dozed fitfully until they arrived at the breakfast station at Gallatin, a little town on the river.

After an hour's rest and a change of horses, they pushed on again. From this point onward they found the reports about the condition of the roads fully verified. The stage lumbered along through the deep, muddy roads, and ever and anon the passengers would be required to alight, and assist in lifting the wheels from a particularly soft spot, where they were threatened with being inextricably mired. As may be imagined, a journey under such circumstances was far from being a pleasant one, but they all submitted with good nature to a state of affairs which was beyond their power to remedy. As it was, they fared much better than a party of travelers whom they met upon the road. They were returning from Helena, and when crossing a narrow bridge over one of the mountain streams, had the misfortune to have their coach overturned, and themselves precipitated violently to the ground, thereby sustaining serious injury. Upon meeting this forlorn party of travelers, Manning and his companions all turned out again, and by Herculean efforts succeeded in righting the overturned coach, and in repairing, as far as in their power, the damage that had been done. With such laborious experiences as these, the party traveled on, and by the time they had arrived at the supper station they were almost exhausted.

After this, however, the roads gradually improved, and as darkness came on, they again essayed to sleep. On they went, and the night was passed in uncomfortable slumber, broken and disturbed by the lurching and uneasy jolting of the coach over the rough mountain roads, and the curses of the driver, administered without stint to the struggling and jaded horses. The night, however, brought neither danger nor mishap, and at four o'clock in the morning they arrived at Helena, very much demoralized and worn out, but with whole bodies and ravenous appetites. Manning went to bed immediately on his arrival, and did not awake until the sun was high in the heavens, when he arose, feeling considerably refreshed and strengthened by his repose.

Helena, the capital of Montana, he found to be a pushing and energetic city of about ten thousand inhabitants. Here were mills and factories, a handsome court-house, graded schools, several newspapers, charitable institutions and public hospitals, in fact, all the progressive elements of a thriving and well-settled city of modern times. All this had been accomplished in less than twenty years, and without the assistance of the railroad or the energizing influence of river navigation. The railroad had not yet penetrated into this mountainous region, and the Missouri river was fourteen miles distant. To the adventurous spirit of gold-hunting Americans had Helena owed its origin and growth, and its resources were unknown until 1864, when a party of prospecting miners discovered unmistakable evidences of rich yielding gold and silver mines in the immediate vicinity of what is now the thriving city of Helena. Following this discovery, thousands of gold-hunters sought this new "Eldorado," and in a few months a populous community had taken possession of the ground. Within a year after this the territory of

Montana was formed, and from its central location and large population, Helena was chosen as the capital. From this time the success of
the city was assured, emigration continued, the mines showed no signs
of diminution, and the town soon aspired to the dignity of a city, despite
its remoteness from the river, the railroad and the telegraph. Exceeding
even California in the richness of its gold mines, Montana shows a
wonderful yield of silver, which is obtained with an ease which makes
mining a pleasurable and sure source of incalculable profit. In addition
to the precious metals, copper is also found in abundance, and forms
an important feature of the mineral wealth of this territory.

Montana is easily reached during the season of navigation by steam-
boats on the Missouri river from St. Louis, from which point, without
obstruction or transshipment, the river is navigable to Fort Benton,
situated almost in the center of the territory, a distance of more than
twenty-five hundred miles. Here, too, there is a large and constant supply
of water, a matter of great difficulty and scarcity in other mining
districts. As the range of the Rocky Mountains in this vicinity does not
present that broken and rugged character which marks the other ranges,
the land is especially adapted for agricultural purposes, and timber of
all kinds abounds in sufficient quantities for all the purposes of home
consumption. Possessing these manifold and important advantages, it
is not strange that the country is not materially dependent upon the
railroads for its growth and present development.

These facts Manning gleaned in a conversation with the proprietor
of the hotel, while he was making his preparations to commence his
search for the man whose crime had led him such a long chase, and
whose detection now seemed hopefully imminent.

Chapter XXII

In Helena — A Fruitless Quest — Jerry Taylor's Bagnio — Reliable
Tidings — A Midnight Ride — Arrival at Butte City.

*A*fter obtaining much valuable information with reference to the various localities of the city, from the landlord of the hotel, Manning sallied forth upon his quest. With untiring energy he prosecuted his inquiries, only to meet with repeated disappointments and rebuffs; all day long he labored assiduously, visiting a hundred brothels, saloons and hotels, and yet without discovering a trace of Duncan or his white-faced quadruped. Could it be possible that the honest-faced miner had played him false, and designedly thrown him off the scent? Might not the saloon-keeper at Bozeman have given him the proper direction of Duncan's flight toward the Yellowstone park? and was he not now miles away from all pursuit, and perhaps by this time fully aware that he was being followed? These thoughts flew through the brain of the detective as after all his efforts he found himself baffled at all points. At length, in despair, he sought the aid of the authorities, and was received with a cordiality that was unmistakable, and with a proffer of assistance that promised to be valuable in the extreme. An officer, well tried and trusted, a man of considerable experience, and who was the very ideal of a discreet and intelligent official, was delegated to accompany him during the evening. For a long time these two men devoted their combined energies to the task before them; but as had been the case with Manning during the day, no success attended their efforts.

At length the officer turned to Manning and said:

"There is only one more place where we can possibly hope to hear from your friend, and I have left that until the last, because I scarcely hope to learn anything even there."

"Let us go at once," said the detective; "drowning men, they say, catch at straws. I am determined that no possible point shall be lost and we may only be disappointed again; but let us try."

"Come along, then," replied the officer; "but keep your revolver where you can find it, for you may have occasion to use it."

"Where are we going?" asked Manning.

"To Jerry Taylor's ranch," answered the officer, "as hard a dive as you ever saw."

"Very well," said Manning, "we will go. I have no fear for myself, and perhaps this is the turning-point in our search."

So saying they started off, and after half an hour's walk found themselves in the extreme northern part of the city, and in a locality which presented anything but an inviting appearance.

Although but a short distance from one of the main thoroughfares, the houses were of the most wretched character, and the people who were congregated about the doorways were villainous looking men and low-browed, brazen-faced women. Lights shone from many windows, and from within came the sound of loud laughter and ribald song. They were evidently in a quarter of the city where vice reigned supreme and where poverty, crime and immorality held full sway.

Passing through this neighborhood without molestation, for Manning's companion seemed to be well known and universally feared, they reached a long, rambling frame building, which was gaily painted and brightly illuminated. Men and women of all ages were entering and leaving the place, and crowds of people were gathered about the entrance. Above the noise of the clinking of glasses and the loud orders of the waiters, could be heard the sounds of music, and a general confusion of voices that bespoke a large assembly.

The detective had frequently heard of the character of a dance-house in the far west, and here was an opportunity to view one in full blast. Elbowing their way through the crowd, Manning and his companion soon found themselves in a large, brilliantly lighted room, almost entirely bereft of furniture. At one end was a raised platform, on which were seated the orchestra, consisting of a piano, sadly out of tune, a cracked violin, and a cornet which effectually drowned out the music of the other two instruments. Around the sides of the room were ranged rows of tables and wooden chairs, which were occupied by men and women, all busily occupied in disposing of the villainous liquids which were dispensed to them by so-called pretty waiter girls, who had evidently long since become strangers to modesty and morality. The band was playing a waltz, and the floor was filled with a motley gathering of both sexes, who were whirling about the room, with the greatest abandonment, dancing madly to the harsh and discordant music. The scene was a perfect pandemonium, while boisterous laughter and loud curses mingled with and intensified the general excitement and confusion.

Both the men and women were drinking freely, and some of them were in a wild state of intoxication, while others had long since passed the stage of excitement and were now dozing stupidly in the corners of the room.

Manning and his companion stood for some time gazing at the scenes around them. The detective's mind was busy with somber meditations upon the human degradation that was here presented. Here were women, many of them still youthful and with marks of beauty still remaining, in spite of their life of dissipation. Their eyes were flashing under the influence of intoxication, and from their pretty lips were issuing blasphemies which made him shudder. Old women, with a long record of shame and immorality behind them, and with their bold faces covered with cosmetics to hide the ravages of time. Rough men, with their flannel shirts and their trousers tucked into their high, mud-covered boots. Young men of the city, dressed well and apparently respectable, yet all yielding to their passion for strong drink and the charms of lewdness and indecency. A strange, wild gathering of all grades and conditions, mingling in a disgraceful orgy which the pen refuses to depict. How many stories of happy homes wrecked and broken could be related by these painted lizards who now were swimming in this whirlpool of licentious gratification! How many men, whose past careers of honor and reputation had been thrown away, were here gathered in this brothel, participating in so-called amusements, which a few years ago would have appalled them! Ah, humanity is a strange study, and debased humanity the strangest and saddest of them all.

The detective was aroused from his reflections by the voice of his companion.

"What do you think of this?"

"I scarcely know," answered Manning, sadly. "I have seen much of the undercurrent of social life, but this exceeds anything I have ever before experienced."

"Oh, this is comparatively nothing," said the other. "Pleasure is the ruling spirit now. You should be here some time when there is a fight, and then you would think that hell was a reality, and these people devils incarnate."

While they were thus conversing, the proprietor of the establishment, Jerry Taylor, approached them, and respectfully saluting the officer, whom he knew, said smilingly:

"Seein' the sights of the city, are you, lieutenant?"

"Well, yes, Jerry; that's part of our business. But we are looking for a young man who was here a few days ago, and perhaps you can help us?"

"Well, if I can do anything for you I will," answered Jerry, who was a tall, broad-shouldered, black-haired man, with flashing black eyes and a somber mustache, which trailed below his chin. "Come over into the wine-room, where we can talk. We can't do it here for the noise."

Accepting the suggestion, the three men walked across the room, and entering a narrow doorway in one corner, were ushered into an apartment which was designated as the "wine-room." This room was occupied by the better dressed portion of the habitués of the place, and their deportment was much more circumspect than those in the larger room outside. Leading the way to a table in a retired corner of the room, the proprietor requested them to be seated, while Manning called for the services of one of the waiter girls in providing for their liquid nourishment.

The officer, who had obtained possession of Duncan's photograph, now produced it, and handing it over to Mr. Taylor, said:

"Jerry, that is the fellow we are looking for. Do you know anything about him?"

Taylor looked at the picture a moment, and then answered:

"Certainly, I know something about him. He was here two or three days ago, and was as flush with his money as a nobby aristocrat."

Manning's heart leaped with joy as he heard these words. He was no longer doubtful of results, and was satisfied that he was upon the right track.

"How long did he stay here?" asked the officer.

"Let me see," said Taylor, meditatingly. "He had a white-faced pony with him, and I took care of the animal in my stable. He was here, I guess, a day and two nights."

"Do you know which way he went?" now inquired Manning.

"Wait a moment, gentlemen," said Taylor, rising to his feet, "I think I can find someone who can tell you all about it."

Walking to the door, he disappeared, and after an absence of a few minutes he returned, accompanied by a rather handsome young woman of about twenty years of age, and who appeared to be far superior to the balance of the females whom Manning had noticed since his entrance into the bagnio.

The young woman came smilingly forward, and seating herself at the table, deliberately poured out a glass of wine, and tossed it off with an air of good humor that proved her to be no novice in the art.

Jerry Taylor introduced the gay cyprian to the officers, and the nature of their business was soon made known to her.

Without hesitation or the faintest evidence of a blush, she informed the officers that Duncan had been her companion during his stay in

Helena, and that they had enjoyed each other's company immensely. He had lots of money, the girl said, and she had assisted him in spending some of it. In reply to their questions, the girl stated that Duncan had left Helena two days ago, and that he intended going to Butte City, where he had relatives in business. Further than this she could not say, and they were compelled to be satisfied with what information she had been able to give them.

This was reliable and satisfactory news to Manning, and after lingering in the place a few minutes longer, and compensating the girl for her revelations, the two men took their departure and returned to the hotel, well pleased with the result of the evening's experience.

Upon making inquiries, Manning learned, to his intense disappointment, that he would be obliged to wait until noon on the following day before he could secure a passage in the stage for Butte City. As no time was to be lost, now that he was approaching so near to what he hoped would be the termination of his journey, Manning determined not to delay his departure until the starting of the coach. The nights were moonlight now, and requesting the further services of the officer in assisting him to procure a good saddle horse and a guide, Manning resolved to start at once for Butte City.

A horse was soon secured, and a trusty man was found who was well acquainted with the road, and who was willing to accompany him. Bidding farewell to the officer, whom he amply remunerated for his trouble, Manning, at ten o'clock that night, leaped into his saddle and set out on his journey. He rode hard all that night, and at sunrise reached Boulder, having traveled considerably more than half the distance. Here they stopped for breakfast, to feed their horses and take some rest. His guide left him at Boulder City and returned to Helena, and about nine o'clock, Manning set off alone for Butte. He pushed on without delay or accident, and about four o'clock in the afternoon arrived at his destination.

His first care was to provide quarters for his horse, and to make arrangements for his return to Helena by the stage next day, after which he sought the hotel for rest, and refreshment for himself.

How near he was to the object of his long search he did not know, but tired and hungry from his long ride, he mentally breathed a prayer that success would speedily crown his efforts, and that the weary chase would soon be ended.

Chapter XXIII

The Long Trail Ended — Duncan Traced to his Lair — Caught at Last — The Escaping Burglar a Prisoner.

*B*utte City is a rich mining village in Deer Lodge county in the territory of Montana, and is surrounded by high hills, which contain rich deposits of gold and silver which are taken from the quartz rock, and in the city are situated the furnaces and other appliances for extracting the precious metals from the rocks in which they are found. The population, although largely of a transient and adventurous character, is composed of a respectable, well-ordered community, many of whom have located permanently, and have labored for the advancement and success of the village. There are several stores, numerous hotels, many very handsome private dwellings, and a newspaper. Though not so large as Helena, by any means, it bids fair in time to rival her more successful neighbor, and the elements of success are found within her domain. The local government consists of a mayor and a city marshal, while the deputies of the latter official constitute the police force who maintain order in the city and protect the persons and property of the citizens. A substantial jail looks frowningly down upon one of the main thoroughfares, and altogether Butte City is as well-conducted and carefully managed a town as is to be found west of the Mississippi river. Within a few months a railroad, a branch of the Union Pacific road, had been completed, which placed the city in communication, both by rail and telegraph, with the larger towns and cities located in the South and East.

After a hearty dinner and a refreshing bath, Manning left the hotel and sought the office of the city marshal. Here, as elsewhere, he was received with the utmost courtesy and kindness, and with a warm proffer of assistance, which the detective most gladly accepted. He detailed the circumstances of the robbery and his long pursuit of the escaping burglar, and also his strong belief that Duncan was now hiding in the city. The marshal fully coincided with his views, and promised to aid him to the utmost of his ability. He then furnished Manning with the address of Duncan's relative, and the detective started out to find the locality to which he had been directed.

He soon discovered the place he was looking for, located on the second floor of one of the larger buildings in the city, and over the entrance was suspended the sign:

George Duncan, Clothier

Mounting the stairs without hesitation, the detective entered the store, where he found to his intense satisfaction the merchant at home. He was assured of this fact from the striking resemblance which the man bore to his fugitive relation. On the pretense of ordering a suit of clothing, the detective engaged him in conversation for some time, and after satisfying himself that Duncan was not about the premises he took his leave, promising to call again and effect his purchase. Arriving on the outside, Manning took up a position where he could watch the entrance unobserved, and where anyone entering or leaving the place could be readily seen by him. Maintaining his watch for several hours, he was gratified, about nine o'clock, to see the clothier making preparations to close his store, and a few moments afterwards he appeared upon the street. As the merchant walked along the streets, the detective followed him closely, never losing sight of him for a moment. For a time the man strolled about, apparently with no definite object in view, and Manning began to fear that his hopes of finding Duncan were futile, and that this relative was entirely unaware of his relative's movements. The night was dark and it was with difficulty that he could keep his man in sight, without approaching so close as to excite suspicion. At last, however, the merchant came out of a saloon which he had entered a short time before, and this time he was accompanied by another man whom Manning could not obtain a fair view of. Taking a circuitous route, they at length gained the main street in the vicinity of the merchant's store. Here they entered a doorway leading from the street and ascending a stairway were soon lost to sight. The detective at once surmised that the clothier occupied sleeping apartments in the building, and that the two men had probably retired for the night.

His first impulse was to follow them upstairs and demand admittance, and should Duncan prove to be one of the parties, to make the arrest then and there. A little reflection, however, convinced him that such a proceeding would be not only unwise but hazardous in the extreme. He was not sure that the companion of the merchant was Duncan, as he had been unable to get close enough to recognize him, and a precipitate entry now would, in case he was not the man, only serve to put them all upon their guard against future surprises.

Manning therefore rapidly made his way to the marshal's office, and finding him within, at once acquainted him with what he had discovered, and requested his advice and assistance. The marshal selected one of his most trusty assistants and the three men repaired to the place where Manning had seen the merchant and his companion enter. The marshal, who was intimately acquainted with the clothing merchant, informed Manning that the gentleman occupied apartments in the building, and suggested that he would be the best man to go up, as in case their man was not there, he could invent some pretext for his visit which would not excite undue suspicion.

This proposition was agreed to, and the marshal ascended the stairs. He found the room unoccupied by the merchant and knocked at the door. All was dark and silent within, and no response came to his summons. After again knocking and making a careful examination of the place, the marshal was convinced that the room was empty and that the men, whoever they were, had departed.

Returning to the sidewalk, a hurried consultation was held, and it was determined to leave the deputy to watch the room, while Manning and the marshal went to the various livery stables in the town, in order to ascertain if Duncan had arrived and had quartered his horse at any of them. This arrangement was immediately carried into execution, and stationing the deputy in a position where he could safely watch the premises, the other two started upon their errand.

To Manning's delight their inquiries were rewarded with success, and at one of the livery stables they found the identical white-faced pony which had carried Duncan on his long journey, and which was now quietly resting in comfortable quarters. This was indeed glad tidings to the indefatigable detective, and he could have caressed the graceful little animal from pure joy. There was now no longer any doubt that Duncan was in the city, and that with proper precautions he could be secured. From Mr. Livermore, it was learned that Duncan had arrived in Butte City on the morning of the day previous, and that he was believed to be making preparations for a trip into Mexico, in company with his cousin, the merchant.

Believing that the best means now to be adopted to secure the young man, was to remain in the stable until Duncan called for his horse, Manning requested permission to do so, which was cheerfully granted by the obliging liveryman. Manning therefore took up his position as a watcher, while the marshal went to look after the man whom they had left on the lookout at the sleeping apartments of the clothing merchant.

After watching for a long time, Manning made himself as comfortable as possible, and prepared to spend the night in his new quarters. He dozed and slept at fitful intervals in his uncomfortable position, and the long night wore away without the appearance of the much-desired visitor.

The stable in which Manning had established himself, was arranged with a row of stalls on either side, with a wide passage-way extending between them. He therefore ensconced himself in the vacant stall immediately opposite to the burglar's horse, and where he could see him at all times. By peering through the crevices in the woodwork he also commanded a full view of the entrance, and was thus enabled to see all who entered the barn. Slowly the morning waned away and as yet no sign of the man for whom he was waiting. How many times he had fancied he heard the longed-for footstep, and peered anxiously out, only to be disappointed, it would be impossible to tell. At length, however, just as he was about to despair of success, he heard footsteps at the door, and peeping through the opening in the stall, he saw the figure of the man for whose appearance he had watched so long, and whose face had haunted him day and night since he had started in pursuit of him. There he stood, not a dozen feet away from him, and as the detective gazed at the unsuspecting thief, a thrill of pleasurable excitement filled his being. In a moment, however, he had controlled himself; and perfectly calm and collected, he watched the man before him. There was no doubt that Duncan was contemplating a renewal of his journey. He was dressed in a hunting suit of heavy brown ducking, with high top boots and a wide brimmed sombrero, while across his shoulders was slung a leather bag, which was filled probably with clothing and provisions. In his hand he carried a splendid repeating rifle, and a brace of pistols were in his belt.

All this the detective was able to note in the brief moment that Duncan paused at the door, as if looking for someone to whom he could give orders for the saddling of his horse. Seeing no one about the place, however, he set his rifle down in a corner by the door, and walked slowly down the passage until he reached the stall where his pony was standing.

He was now directly in front of the spot where the detective was concealed, but with his back toward the operative. As he turned to go into the stall, Manning stopped quickly forward, with his revolver in his hand, and grasping Duncan firmly by the shoulder, he said:

"Thomas Duncan, I have caught you at last."

Duncan started as though he had been shot, as these words rang in his ears, and he felt the grasp of the detective's strong arm. In an instant he recovered himself, and his hand quickly sought one of the revolvers in his belt. The detective, however, was too quick for him, and placing the muzzle of his pistol against the burglar's cheek, he said, determinedly:

"If you attempt to draw your pistol, I'll blow your brains out!"

Duncan felt that it was useless to attempt to trifle with the resolute man before him, and his arms dropped to his side.

"It's no use, Tod," said Manning, with a quiet smile. "I've got the drop on you, and you might as well cave. Throw your pistols on the ground."

Mechanically Duncan did as he was directed, and then turning to Manning, he inquired in a low, suppressed tone:

"What do you want me for?"

"For the Geneva bank robbery," answered Manning. "You have led me a pretty long chase, but you see I have caught you at last."

"If you had been one hour later," said the other, doggedly, "you never would have taken me. Once on my horse, I would have defied you, and I would have killed you like a dog."

"Well, well," answered Manning, "we won't talk about what you might have done. I've got you, and that's enough for me."

At this juncture the marshal made his appearance, and offering his assistance, the crestfallen young burglar was quietly led away to the jail, where he was searched, and fifteen hundred dollars in money was found upon his person, besides an excellent and valuable gold watch. Without waiting for any further results, Manning rushed to the telegraph office, in order to apprise me of his success. He could not repress a pardonable feeling of pride in the victory he had accomplished. His search was ended, his man was a prisoner, and shortly afterward there came clicking over the wires to Chicago, the following message:

"I have him, fifteen hundred dollars in money, a gold watch, horse and rifle. Will sell horse for what I can get, and leave here, with prisoner, for Chicago, in the morning."

Chapter XXIV

The Burglar Returns to Chicago — Revelations by the Way — The Missing Five Thousand Dollars.

*A*s I had received no tidings of John Manning since his departure from Minneapolis, it may be imagined that I was considerably relieved when his brief but comprehensive telegram from Butte City was received. So long a time had elapsed since he had been able to transmit me any definite information about his movements, that I had begun to grow alarmed, not only for the successful termination of his pursuit, but for his personal safety. Now, however, all my fears were set at rest; the daring and ambitious detective was safe and well, and in addition to this he had succeeded in capturing the fugitive, who was now in his custody. The chase had been a long and fatiguing one, but victory had crowned our efforts, and the entire quartette of criminals were now in the hands of the officers of the law, and would be held to answer for their crimes. The pursuit of Duncan had been most admirably carried out by my trusted operative, and Manning was deserving of unstinted credit for the sagacious mind and untiring spirit he displayed. So thoroughly determined had he been to secure his prisoner, that no consideration of personal comfort, or even necessary rest, had been allowed to interfere with his movements. With more than a month elapsing between the commission of the crime and the commencement of the chase, and traveling over a country thinly settled and semi-barbarous, I regarded the victory which he had achieved as one deserving of the highest encomiums, and reflecting great credit upon his skill, determination and pertinacity.

Mr. Silby and the bank officials were immediately notified of Duncan's capture, and their satisfaction was unbounded; their congratulations were unsparingly uttered, and their words of commendation were of the heartiest and warmest character. They were now fully satisfied that the vexing problem of the missing five thousand dollars in coin would be solved, and earnestly hoped that the solution would inure to their advantage. However, nothing could be done in the matter until the arrival of Duncan, and we impatiently awaited his appearance.

The next morning after his arrest Duncan was placed on the train, and in company with John Manning started for Chicago. The detective had experienced no difficulty in disposing of the horse owned by the young prisoner, and Mr. Livermore, the stable-man, became his purchaser for a fair price. Having experienced quite as much of the discomforts and fatigues of traveling by stagecoach and on horseback as he desired, Manning resolved to return to Chicago by rail, and he accordingly took passage on the Idaho division of the Union Pacific railroad, which would be both a more expeditious and comfortable mode of traveling, besides being a safe method of conducting a prisoner.

Ever since his arrest Duncan had been sullen and uncommunicative. He was evidently crushed by the sudden and surprising turn which affairs had taken. In the moment of his triumph he had fallen, and when he fancied himself the most secure, defeat and detection had overtaken him. It was not long, however, after they had started upon their return journey, ere Manning succeeded in breaking through his reserve, and in inducing him to talk freely. To the young man's credit be it said, that the first inquiry he made was in regard to the recovery of Miss Patton, the young lady whom he had assaulted in the bank, and when he learned of her speedy and complete recovery, he seemed quite relieved. He expressed the most intense regret at having been compelled, as he put it, to treat her so roughly, and he added, "I tell you she was a plucky little woman, and had Eugene Pearson been an honest man and fought as well as she did, we never could have got that money."

"She is certainly a brave girl," replied Manning.

"Why, look here," exclaimed Duncan, extending his left hand toward him, upon two fingers of which the detective noticed several dark-looking and freshly-healed scars. "I was compelled to strike her. She fastened her teeth into my hand, and bit me to the bone. I never could have got loose without that; as it was, my hand bled terribly, and was a long time in healing, besides being excessively painful."

By degrees the detective led him to speak of his connection with the robbery, and after a momentary hesitation he revealed the whole story, which in every particular coincided with that already told by Newton Edwards. He stated that being in Chicago without money, and without a friend except Edwards, he had requested a loan from him, which was readily granted. Then followed another drinking spree in company with his friend, and during its continuance Edwards proposed the robbery, and explained how easily and safely it might be accomplished. Lured by the glittering prospect and intoxicated as he was, he gave a ready consent to enter into the scheme, and almost before he was aware of it, and certainly before he became thoroughly sober, the burglary had been committed, and with his ill-gotten gains he was on the road, seeking to escape from the consequences of his crime. He professed sincere repentance for what he had done, and stated that this was his first offense, which would now have to be atoned for by a long term of imprisonment.

As they progressed upon their way, and when about fifty miles out, Duncan informed the detective that he had met a noted rough in Butte City who was known as Texas Jack, and that this man had told his cousin that, if he desired it, a party could be raised, who would waylay the train and effect his rescue.

"What would you have done if they had made the attempt?" asked Duncan, jocularly.

"Well," answered Manning coolly, and with determination, "they might have taken you, but it would have been after I had put a bullet through your brain."

The quiet and resolute tone in which this was said, caused the robber's cheek to turn pale, as he saw the determined spirit of the man with whom he had to deal. It is needless to say that no attempt was made to effect a rescue, nor had Manning any fears that such an effort would be made, but he deemed it wise to give his prisoner a quiet but firm hint as to what the consequences would be if a rescue was attempted.

During the remainder of the journey Duncan was as cheerful and pleasant in his manner as though no thought of a prison entered his mind, and the detective experienced no trouble or annoyance with him whatever.

Two days later they arrived at Council Bluffs, where they changed cars, and, taking the Rock Island route, they were not long in reaching Chicago. Manning brought his prisoner to my agency, where he was taken care of until arrangements could be made for his transportation to Geneva.

I cannot express the satisfaction I experienced when I realized at last that our chase was over, and that a full and satisfying victory had attended our efforts in this matter. All of the prisoners were now taken, and, except for the solution of the question of the missing five thousand dollars, our work had been successfully accomplished.

Another matter Duncan had related to Manning while upon their journey, which, while unfortunate for us, at the same time did not detract from the victory we had gained. It appeared that, while traveling from Bozeman to Helena, Duncan had occasion to use his pocket-handkerchief, and, in pulling it out of his pocket, he also drew out a small package of notes which he carried loosely in his pocket, and which contained nearly five hundred dollars. This was exceedingly unfortunate, and accounted in some measure for the small amount of money which was found upon Duncan's person at the time of his capture.

However, this was of comparatively trifling importance, when the important features of his arrest are considered, and when even the amount of fifteen hundred dollars had been actually recovered.

On the whole, I was very well contented with affairs as they were, and as far as the bank was concerned, there was every indication of thankfulness and rejoicing.

Chapter XXV

The Mystery of the Missing Five Thousand Dollars Solved at Last — The Money Recovered — Duncan at Geneva.

On the day following the arrival of Duncan in Chicago, he was conveyed to Geneva, in company with my son William and a trusty operative. As may be imagined, the appearance of the fourth and hitherto unknown burglar threw the inhabitants of the quiet little town into another state of wild excitement, this time, however, without any indication of hostility to my officers or their actions. A charge of sentiment had taken place in the public mind, and now, instead of threatened resistance to our movements, my men were received with every evidence of approbation and endorsement.

Thomas Duncan was taken at once to the bank and here he made a full statement of his connection with the robbery, the amount of money which he and Newton Edwards obtained, and detailed at length his travels from the time he left Geneva until he was arrested at Butte City by John Manning. He fully corroborated the statement of Newton Edwards about their disappointment in not obtaining, within five thousand dollars, as much money as they expected, and he expressed the belief that Eugene Pearson had taken this additional sum, and had thus deceived both his companions and the bank.

He fully explained the disposition they made of the valise, which contained the silver, by hiding it in the corn-field by the roadside; after which they continued their journey unencumbered by the weight of the coin, which they did not consider valuable enough to burden themselves with.

After he had finished, William inquired:

"Was there no other sack or sacks than those you have mentioned as being in the valise when you threw it away? Did you not dispose of some before you parted with the satchel? Think carefully now; there is a mystery about that sack of gold which we want to solve, if possible."

"Eugene Pearson declares," added Mr. Silby, the bank president, "that he has given up everything, and is positive that you took away from the bank nearly fifteen thousand dollars in currency and coin."

Again, as in the case of Edwards, the valise was brought out, and the amount of money which was supposed to have been taken at the time of the robbery, less five thousand dollars in gold, was handed to Duncan to lift. Duncan raised it in his hand, and at once pronounced it lighter than when they carried it away from the bank. A sack containing five thousand dollars in gold was then added, and when he again took it in his hands, he exclaimed:

"That's more like it; when we left the bank the valise was fully that heavy."

"Now, Mr. Duncan," said Mr. Silby, "this test satisfies me that Eugene Pearson is innocent of having taken more money than he has restored to us, and that when you left the bank, you carried away the amount he states."

While Mr. Silby was speaking, Duncan had been recalling all the events which had transpired during their flight, and endeavoring to trace, step by step, all that they had done.

"I remember now," he said slowly, after a few moments, "that before we concluded to throw away the valise, we sat down by the railroad track to rest. We then opened the valise, to see what it contained. Among the contents, I noticed a small, dingy sack, which was marked 'silver — $100,' and that being pretty heavy, and only a small amount, I took it and hid it in the weeds that were growing around us. I suppose it is there yet, provided no one has found and removed it."

At this juncture, Mr. Welton, the cashier, who had been listening quietly, jumped to his feet and excitedly exclaimed:

"That solves the mystery! I remember distinctly having placed that gold in a sack marked silver, as it was the only one we could find at the time." Then turning to Duncan, he added: "You, therefore, instead of throwing away one hundred dollars in silver, as you supposed, actually disposed of five thousand dollars in as good gold as ever came from the mint."

This explanation appeared to be as plain as the sun at noonday, and it was evident that, mistaking the contents of the sack to be silver, and of a small amount, Duncan had thrown it away, not deeming it worth the trouble of taking.

"Can you tell the spot where you disposed of this sack?" asked William, who still indulged in the hope of recovering the missing money.

"I think I could find it," answered Duncan. "And if you gentlemen will accompany me, I think I can point it out to you."

Without delay, a carriage was procured, and Mr. Silby, Mr. Welton, Duncan and my son William, started off. They proceeded in the direction which Duncan said they had traveled after leaving the bank, and without difficulty he found the spot where he said they had stopped to rest.

Alighting from the carriage, Duncan pointed out the place where they had seated themselves, and he sat down in what he claimed was the exact spot. It was at the foot of a little bank, which rose abruptly from the roadside, and was covered thickly with heavy grass and weeds, now dry and withered, and closely packed together. The three men who accompanied Duncan grew exceedingly anxious at this point, for a few moments would decide the question of the recovery of a large amount of money, or its unquestionable loss. Silently they waited, as Duncan thrust his hand under this growth of dry grass and weeds, where he said he had put the gold, and with surprise and joy they saw him draw forth the identical dingy-looking canvas bag. Exultantly he held it aloft, and then placed it in the hands of Mr. Welton, who, on opening it, found the shining gold pieces, and the mystery of the missing money was solved at last.

During all the weeks that had elapsed since the robbery, that gold had lain there undisturbed. Hundreds and thousands of people had tramped over the ground in the hope of finding some traces of the burglars, and no one had discovered the snug little sum which lay so temptingly near them, and which might have been theirs for the simple trouble of taking it.

As for the bank officials and ourselves, our gratification at this profitable discovery was only exceeded by our astonishment at the singular manner in which it had been at last accomplished. Then, too, it set at rest all doubts as to the truthfulness of young Pearson's story, and proved conclusively that he was honestly regretful and penitent for the crime he had committed, and had given up all he had taken. At the same time it relieved his companions from any suspicion of having made away with or concealed it for future use.

As for Duncan, to his credit it must be added, that he seemed as much pleased and relieved at this restoration of the stolen money as did any of the others, and this action impressed the officers of the bank with a feeling of profound sympathy for the unfortunate young man, and convinced them that although he had been guilty of a serious crime, he was not really bad at heart, and that this was his first offense, into which he had been led by his thoughtless folly and reckless dissipation. At his request, he was allowed to see Miss Patton, and to her he frankly and feelingly expressed his regrets for having so roughly treated her, and her forgiving words were received as gratefully as could have been desired.

Our work was nearly finished. Out of twenty thousand dollars which had been taken, we had succeeded in recovering nearly eighteen thousand dollars; the balance, having been squandered by Edwards and Duncan, was, of course, irretrievably gone. But this was good enough as it was, and the officers of the bank were satisfied and delighted at this most satisfactory conclusion of an operation which, at its commencement, promised so little, and out of which such great results had flowed.

The party returned to Geneva, and the next day Duncan was formally arraigned. He waived an examination, and in default of bail was removed to the county prison, where his confederates were already confined, anxiously awaiting their trial.

Chapter XXVI

Conclusion — Retribution.

A few days later, and the last act in this sad drama of crime was performed. The four youthful criminals were arraigned for trial before a conscientious judge, and by a jury composed of gentlemen, many of whom were intimately acquainted with two of the accused, Eugene Pearson and Dr. Johnson, both of whom, it will be remembered, were born and reared in the little town of Geneva. As may be imagined, the trial attracted universal attention in that section of the country, and on the day that the court was convened, the town was filled with people from all the surrounding districts, who came to witness the important proceedings. Long before the hour fixed for the commencement of the trial, the court-room was crowded to suffocation by the eager multitude, who had come from far and near, for the purpose of being present at this unusual judicial investigation. Many were actuated only by the promptings of idle curiosity, and regarded the trial somewhat in the light of a diverting exhibition, for which no admission fee was charged; others, from a stern sense of justice, came to view a trial in which crime was to be punished, and the law in all its majesty was to be invoked for the protection of the honor of society, and the property of the individual. There was yet another class, who came from the impulses of love and sympathy and friendship — some who were linked to the unfortunate criminals by the ties of family and blood, and some who had known and esteemed them ere their hearts had been hardened, and before the wiles of the tempter had lured them from the paths of honor and virtue. There were present also the grey-haired father and mother of Eugene Pearson, broken and bowed with the grief and shame which had been brought upon them by the crimes of their beloved son; the aged parents of Dr. Johnson, who had come to witness, with saddened hearts, the doom of their darling boy; the young wife of Newton Edwards, who in the moment of her husband's ruin had, with true womanly devotion, forgotten his past acts of cruelty and harshness, and now, with aching heart and tear-stained eyes, was waiting, with fear and trembling, to hear the dreaded judgment pronounced upon the man whom she had sworn to "love and cherish" through "good and evil report."

Since his incarceration she had been a constant visitor to his cell, and by her love and sympathy had sought to uphold the fallen man in the dark hours of his shame and disgrace. Here also was the aged father of Thomas Duncan, the only friend whom the young man had in all that vast assembly. Though his face was stern and immovable, yet the quivering of the lips and the nervous trembling of the wrinkled hands told too plainly that he too was suffering beyond expression in the sorrow that had been wrought by the boy who in his early years had been his pride and joy.

When the judge had taken his seat, and the door opened to admit the four youthful prisoners, all eyes were turned upon them. Slowly and with downcast eyes they entered the chamber of justice, and amid an awelike stillness that pervaded the room, took their seats in the prisoners' dock. In spite of all that had transpired, and with the full conviction that these youthful offenders richly merited whatever judgment they were to receive, there was not one in that entire audience, whose heart did not throb with sympathy for the aged parents and relatives of the accused, and even for the culprits themselves in this, the dreadful hour of their humiliation and grief.

The trial was not a protracted one. A jury was speedily empanelled, the low, stern tones of the judge were heard in timely admonition, and the prosecution was commenced. Upon the prisoners being asked to plead to the indictments which had been prepared against them, Mr. Kirkman, a prominent attorney of Geneva, who had been retained to defend the unfortunate young men, arose, and in impressive tones entered a plea of guilty. With the keen perceptions of a true lawyer, he felt that the proofs were too strong to be overcome, and that to attempt to set up any technical defense would only result in greater hardships to his clients. He, however, made an eloquent and touching appeal for the exercise of judicial clemency. He referred in feeling terms to the youth of the prisoners, to the groups of weeping and stricken relatives, whose prayerful hearts were echoing his appeals. He urged that the evidences of sincere repentance had been manifested by all of the prisoners, and that, as this had been their first offense, the exercise of gentle mercy would be both grand and productive of good results.

His words were not lost even upon the prosecuting attorney, and when Mr. Kirkman had concluded, that gentleman arose, and in a few words echoed the sentiments of the attorney for the defense. He also expressed the conviction that, while justice called loudly for sentence, yet there were elements in this case in which the wisest judgment would be that which partook of the qualities of mercy.

At the conclusion of this request, the judge, with a delicate regard for the tender feelings of the assembled relatives, ordered an adjournment of the court, in order that he might take the merits of the case under advisement, and to enable him to administer such sentence, as, in his best judgment, was demanded under the circumstances. Slowly the immense audience dispersed, and for a few moments the prisoners were allowed to converse with their weeping friends, after which they were again conducted to their cells to await the action of the court.

A few days later they were brought quietly before the judge and their sentences were pronounced. Dr. Johnson, owing to the existence of a doubt as to his complicity in the robbery, was condemned to four years' imprisonment on the charge of forgery, while Newton Edwards, Eugene

Pearson, and Thomas Duncan were each sentenced to an imprisonment of six years on the indictment for burglary.

Thus ended this important case, and the action of the court received the almost universal approbation of the community, while the relatives and nearest friends of the prisoners were compelled to acknowledge its fairness and justice.

But little remains to be told. The prisoners were soon conducted to the state prison, and a short time afterward, having occasion to visit that institution, I saw them again. They all bore evidences of the most acute remorse and contrition, and their life in prison had produced serious effects upon their robust persons. Far different was their lot now, to the free and happy existence which had once been theirs. Eugene Pearson, the dapper young gentleman, was put at hard labor in the stone-cutting department; Johnson, the dentist, was assigned to the machine shop, while Edwards and Duncan were working in the shoe-making department. Day after day the weary labor was performed, and night after night the gloom of the prison cell enshrouds them. Weeks will roll into months and the months will stretch into weary years, ere they will breathe the sweet air of liberty again. Within the frowning walls of the prison, they are paying the heavy penalty for their crime, and here we must leave them, in the earnest and sincere hope that true repentance may come to them, and that when their term of servitude is ended, they may come forth, filled with resolves to live down the stain upon their characters, and by upright and honorable lives to redeem and obliterate the dark and painful past. That "judgment overcometh crime," has been fully proven in the lives of these men, and trusting in the future to redeem the past, we leave them to the burdens and the solitude to which they have brought themselves.

THE END

www.ingramcontent.com/pod-product-compliance
Lightning Source LLC
Chambersburg PA
CBHW050800250626
47155CB00005B/2149